T0343579

SAINTS RESTS

ALSO BY LUKE FRANCIS BEIRNE

*Foxhunt,* 2021
*Blacklion,* 2023

Luke Francis Beirne

# SAINTS REST

Baraka
Books

Montréal

© 2025 Luke Francis Beirne

ISBN 978-1-77186-379-7 pbk; 978-1-77186-385-8 epub; 978-1-77186-386-5 pdf

Cover by Leila Marshy
Cover painting "Fog Lifting" by Cliff Turner
Book Design by Folio infographie
Editing: Leila Marshy
Proofreading: Anne Marie Marko

Legal Deposit, 1st quarter 2025
Bibliothèque et Archives nationales du Québec
Library and Archives Canada

Published by Baraka Books of Montreal
Printed and bound in Quebec

TRADE DISTRIBUTION & RETURNS

Canada
UTPdistribution.com

United States
Independent Publishers Group: IPGbook.com

We acknowledge the support from the Société de développement des entreprises culturelles (SODEC) and the Government of Quebec tax credit for book publishing administered by SODEC.

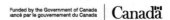

For my mom, Eilish Cleary
(1963-2024).

Mom, I love you.

The clouds scud, tattered by the wind, across a limpid ground. If I had the patience to wait, I would see the moon. But I have not. Now that I have looked, I hear the wind. I close my eyes and it mingles with my breath. Words and images run riot in my head, pursuing, flying, clashing, merging, endlessly. But beyond this great tumult there is a great calm, and a great indifference, never really to be troubled by anything again.

Samuel Beckett, *Malone Dies*

PART I

In Saint John, sunshine was rare. When day broke, the sky turned grey and shards of light glared through to front steps where people huddled and smoked, to dockyards where people worked, to park benches where people slept. In the city's peripheries—the east and west—people sat in breakfast nooks and morning rooms, and maybe the sun shone there, rising over pine-crested cliffs and frozen bays as bacon sizzled in the pan and accounts were discussed, as affairs ended in lawsuits and bitter resentment rather than fistfights and broken windows; but, in the heart, Saint John woke when the light shifted and darkness retreated behind the clouds, distant but ever-present, looming over the uneven rise of flattop roofs.

In our office, Randy and I were wide awake. I hunched over a space heater beside the corner window with a double double and a folder of surveillance photos suggesting that Dustin Colter could walk on his left foot and was, therefore, ineligible for worker's comp. Randy sat at his desk writing up the delicate details of an infidelity case.

Our office was on the third floor of a townhouse on Princess Street. The ceilings were tall and the windows narrow. From the corner, you could see over the curve of the road to the plateau of the harbour, where the fog gathered and rolled.

Below was the South End. Cannery Row, by another name. In the South End, people were real; ghostly demarcations kept apparitions at bay. I sipped the coffee and looked out. It wasn't good but it was familiar.

Footsteps in the hallway stopped in front of the door, drawing a slouching silhouette behind the glass. When the door opened, a woman stood in front of us. Looking forty or way past it, she had distinct smile lines at the upper edge of her mouth, though it didn't appear that they'd had much exercise lately.

The woman was worn, beaten. She wore an old, fur-lined puffer coat: once expensive, now stained and torn.

"Can I help you, ma'am?" Randy asked. He set down his pen, looking her up and down as he did.

The woman glanced at me, then back to Randy. "Is this the Cormier Agency?" She spoke with the rasp of a lifelong smoker.

Randy couldn't help but smile. "It is," he said. He closed the file on his desk. "I'm Randy Cormier. Come on in."

Randy was a good guy. I felt a kind of obligation to him because I was his first employee and he hired me before we even met. The woman looked at me again and closed the door. She was nervous.

Randy gestured to the chair in front of his desk. "Take a seat." She began to unzip her jacket but he lifted his hand. "You might want to leave your coat on," he said. "Landlord controls the heat."

She sat down and folded her arms in her lap, pulling the palms of her hands into her sleeves. Yellow fingertips protruded from the ends.

"What can we do for you?" Randy asked.

I set my coffee on the spare desk in the corner and sat behind it. I opened the folder and began to sort through the photos inside. When Randy's at work, I like to fade into the background. That's where I feel most comfortable, the background.

"My daughter-in-law is missing," the woman said.

"Ok. When was she last seen?" Randy asked.

"Over a year ago."

Randy nodded. He opened the top drawer of his desk and took out a thin black binder. He flipped to an empty sheet. "I'm going to start taking some notes," he said, "in case we open a file. I won't charge you unless we take you on."

She nodded.

"What's your name?" Randy began, filling in the blanks at the top of the sheet.

"Malory Fleet."

I looked up. I did not know Malory but I knew her name. More importantly, I knew the case she was bringing us.

In 2015, on the night of Halloween, her son Jason Fleet was shot to death outside his apartment. No charges were ever laid. Jason was not much missed by the Saint John Police Department. One year to the day, his girl-friend, Amanda Foster, was reported missing.

For a while, the coincidence brought attention to the case. Then it faded into obscurity, relegated to unsolved mystery forums and half-hearted Facebook posts appealing for information.

Randy glanced over at me and then returned his gaze to the woman. "And your daughter-in-law is?"

"Amanda Foster."

Randy set down his pen. "So, they've had no luck then?"

"The police don't give a shit. They're crooked," Malory said. "That's why I'm here."

"Are you in contact with her family?"

"You're looking at her family."

Randy nodded. "Ok," he said. "Malory, listen. A missing family member is usually an easy enough case, a simple matter of asking around. An investigation like this though, with the complicating factors—your son, the ongoing investigation, the police—it could get complicated. It might take a lot of time." He paused. "It might be expensive."

"You don't think I can afford it."

"That's no reflection of yourself," Randy said, exhaling loudly. "I don't think I could afford it."

Malory shrugged. "Cut me loose when my cheques bounce."

For a while, Randy just looked at her, contemplating. Then he nodded. "Ok," he said. "Let's open a file. Talk to me."

On October 31st, 2015, Malory sat on the front porch of a two-story apartment building on Elgin Street, over in the North End. She sat with two neighbours, Bill Comeau and Olivia James. Olivia worked at the Shoppers in the Lansdowne Plaza and Bill worked on the West Side Docks. The first few trick or treaters began trickling through the streets. A bowl of candy rested on the rotting wood at their feet.

"The boys'll be gettin' rowdy tonight," Bill said.

Malory followed his eyes across the road to a back porch where four teenagers sat around a well-used patio set, drinking Colt 45s and smoking Pom-Poms loosely packed with skunk weed. A broken screen door leaned against the wall behind them. The tinny phone speaker struggled with heavy bass. She thought of her son who, just a few years before, might have been one of those boys sitting on the porch. A crow on the wire above shook its wings and took flight.

It was getting darker. Children flowed along the sidewalks, trailing groups of parents. A young boy dressed as Iron Man sprinted down the centre of the street. His mother shook her head and looked around at the other parents, embarrassed by his freedom or her unwillingness to shackle it.

Malory took a sip of her Alpine and set it down on the chipped paint of the railing. When Jason was young, he'd dressed as Spiderman four years in a row. He refused to try anything else. He just saw something in Spiderman that clicked and drew him in.

Bill took a fresh pack of Next cigarettes from his pocket and unwrapped the plastic. He turned one upside down and pulled another out and set it between his lips. He put the pack on the railing and fished in his pockets for a lighter. Children laughed and the cold crisp of Fall set in. Mothers and fathers talked in clustered cells. Somewhere around the corner, an engine roared and tires squealed. Leaves scraped across the asphalt, swirling in the wind.

Olivia waved to someone who passed. She reached down and pulled another beer from the six-pack beside her. The cans were neatly nestled. A group of kids approached a house across the road. Malory watched them. There was a Star Wars character, a minion, and a superhero—a survey of that summer's box office. They looked nervous. It must have been their first house of the night. Children stopped in front of her own porch and her attention shifted.

"Trick or Treat!"

Bill shifted his cigarette into his left hand and lifted the bowl of candy with the right. "Here ya go," he said. "Take as many as ya want."

Excited hands plunged into the bowl. Malory's phone rang. She drew it from her pocket and looked at the screen. It was Amanda.

Malory stopped talking. By then, I was sitting on the desk beside them, listening closely. I thought that Randy might send me away, ask for some privacy, but he didn't. Malory was a natural storyteller, details and all. She had us on the hook. It made me a little wary but I was lapping it up.

"That's when you heard about Jason?" I asked.

Malory looked at me, sizing me up properly for the first time. "Yeah," she said. "That's when she told me about Jason. Three shots. All in the chest. She was inside making popcorn."

"She called you before she called the cops?"

"She did."

"Why?"

"You're the detective. See if you can figure that out," Malory said. She drew her hands back into the sleeves of her jacket, trying to keep the cold at bay. Like that, she wasn't the storyteller anymore. She was a frightened and worn-down woman, a mother.

Randy put down his pen and leaned across the desk. "So, you're here about Amanda," he said. "Not Jason."

"I know what happened to Jason," Malory said.

"You do?" Randy asked. He glanced at me. The case was still open—unsolved.

"Yeah," Malory said, "he died."

"You aren't interested in finding out who killed him?" Randy asked.

"I've already been through that," Malory said. "I just want to find my daughter."

Randy leaned back in the chair and looked at the woman, and then looked at me. "Well, I'll tell you, you cast and I'm biting." He ran his hand over his brow, wiping away some invisible irritant. "But this won't be easy."

"If it was easy, I wouldn't be here," Malory said.

"Touché."

I became a private investigator out of circumstance rather than desire. I went to the police academy right out of high school and realized on the first day that it was a mistake. We were marched in right away. We weren't yet fitted for our uniforms so we wore whites—a simple white shirt and dress pants. We sat in rows of crew-cuts while the director stood above us. He told us that we would be broken down and built back up again. On the eager faces around me, I saw the will to be broken. For thirty-four weeks, I was never alone. For thirty-four weeks, I felt true loneliness for the first time. I learned hatred and fear. I learned to fight and shoot. I learned to take care of our own.

When the course ended, my desire to be a cop lay in shreds. I was broken down, alright—I just hadn't been built back up. I took a security job at a remote camp up north. The solitude was fine and I sat out beneath the stars and the northern lights watching the snow stretch into the distance. On that vast plane, time seemed like it could hold forever if you allowed it to. It's the slant of light, someone once told me, of winter afternoons. Shadows cast longer across the snow. It's the sound too. Everything above the powdery water-line—

the cry of a bird, the crack of an axe or rifle—
stretches across the sky, spreading out through
the empty silent air, hard and clear.

The pay was good and the work was min-
imal but, eventually, I longed for the ocean
wind and the bite of salt in the air. I found a
listing for a company in Saint John, applied,
received an offer, and accepted. I found myself
on Princess Street investigating insurance
claims, helping the rich stay rich and the poor
stay hungry. In Saint John, I met a woman,
Madison. She convinced me to stay. She was
a teller at the bank so our work was the same.
When she left, habit kept me.

Malory walked out of the room and closed the
door. "What do you think?" Randy asked me.
He was chewing on the end of his pen like a
dog with a bone stripped clean.

It was still cold but I could hear the heater
coming to life through the wall. "It's a good
case," I said.

"She can't really afford it." He looked down
at the sheet on the desk. "It's a risk."

"It could be a big break," I said. "Could lead
to bigger things. Missing persons. Not just
surveillance and corporate stuff."

"Surveillance and corporate stuff pays the bills."

I shrugged and sipped the double double.

"What are you working on?"

"The Colter case, the worker's comp."

Randy scratched his head. Thin grey strands fell over his brow. He was older than me by about ten years. He fell into investigative work when his home security store went under. It was no longer the era of brick and mortar.

"Ok," he said. "Finish that off and then go ask around. See what you can find out about the girl. Talk to the cops but be wary. They may have something to hide." He paused. "And they won't like you working their case."

I stood up and tried not to smile. I took my jacket off the back of the chair and slipped it on, grabbed the coffee and walked out. I was already drawn in. When I reached the bottom of the stairs and stepped outside, I saw Malory in the entryway with a cigarette between her cracked lips. Her arms were crossed over her torso for warmth. She nodded to me.

"Where do you live?" I asked.

"North," she said. She spoke around the cigarette, performing acrobatics.

"You got a car?"

She shook her head. "I called a cab." Wisps of smoke left her lips with the words.

"Want a drive?"

"You going that way?"

I wasn't but it seemed like an opportunity and I've learned that, in my business, opportunities can't be passed up. "Close enough," I said.

"Ok, sure. Thanks."

"I'm just down the block." I stepped out onto the sidewalk and she followed me to my minivan, grey and dull. In a job like mine, you have to keep things simple. I took the key from my pocket, unlocked the van, and opened the door.

She stood beside the hood finishing the cigarette.

"Don't worry about it," I said. "Just put down the window."

I got in and shut the door. Malory did the same, tossing Tim Hortons wrappers off the seat and onto the floor beside some empty cups.

"Sorry about that," I said. She shrugged. She lowered the window as I turned the key. I pulled out onto the street. The minivan jolted and rattled over the uneven and cracked road. When I turned at the corner and went up to Union, a police car on the prowl slowed at the intersection, sweeping the grid.

Malory drew on the cigarette, then tapped ash out the open window. The air was cold. She blew a cloud of smoke and watched me drive. "What's your deal?" she asked. "Were you a cop, or something?"

"No," I said. "Private security."

She nodded. "You from Saint John?"

"New Glasgow. Nova Scotia." I pulled onto the bridge and drove over to the north end. I was still new to the city and it wasn't home yet. I didn't know if it ever would be. "Just tell me where to go," I said.

"Keep going for now."

"What do you think happened to Amanda?" I asked. I find that it's best to be direct—most of the time, at least. Not always in the darker cases.

"I don't know." She tossed the butt of the cigarette out the window and rolled it up. "That's why I came to you."

"I asked what you think, not what you know."

"Turn at the lights," she said, pointing.

I followed her directions. "Do you think she's alive?"

"Yeah," she said.

"Do you think it's connected to Jason?"

Malory watched the buildings roll past, the grey light playing across her face. She watched the people on the streets. "Yeah, I do," she said. She pointed again. "Turn here."

I turned the wheel at the corner. "You think it's connected, but you want us to look into Amanda and not Jason? Even though no one was ever charged?"

"Jason's dead," she said. "I already know that. I want to find Amanda. I lost them both when I only had to lose one."

I looked across at her. There was something odd in the phrasing. I wondered what it was like for her, for a mother. She was younger than my own but she reminded me of her in some ways—a distorted reflection who had experienced total loss.

"That's it there," she said. "The blue building. Anywhere here is fine."

It was a light blue duplex with a sagging roof. Paint curled from the slats. I pulled up across the street and Malory opened the door. "Thanks," she said.

"I'll be in touch."

She got out and looked both ways, then crossed the street. She hugged her jacket close and went up the front steps and opened the door. I sat in the van for a while with the soft heat blowing through plastic vents, then pulled back onto the road and looped around the block. It was going to be a tough case.

On the other side of the block, I pulled out my phone and dialed. I waited, watching a man struggle to push a shopping cart through a pile of snow at the corner. Madison used to have a friend that lived somewhere near here. Struggle was a familiar scene. Sometimes I missed the peace and emptiness of the north. Winter there was not a burden. There, it was open and vast. Here, it's shopping carts and slush.

The phone rang twice, then he answered: "Hello?"

"Tommy, it's Frank."

"Hey, buddy. What's up? Sorry, I'm outside on the job here. It's cold as shit. I couldn't read the screen."

Tommy wasn't a friend, exactly. He was a guy I'd known at the academy in Summerside. Chance or circumstance put us both in Saint John. Partnership benefited us both.

"I'm working a case," I said. "I'm looking for Amanda Foster."

"Amanda Foster?" Tommy asked. "Same girl I'm thinking of?"

"Yeah," I said. "She's been missing about a year."

"Yeah," Tommy said. "Little over a year. This is a messy case, buddy. You boys sure you know what you're getting into?"

"We're not interested in the murder," I said. "Just looking for the girl. It's a missing persons thing."

"What do you need?"

"Who worked the Fleet case? On your end."

There was a pause on the other end of the line. "I thought you weren't interested in the murder."

"The cop might know something about the girl. She was tied up in all that."

"I don't know," Tommy said. "I can't remember." There was another pause, longer this time. "Look, buddy, I gotta go. We found a dead guy here at the park. Propped up against the fountain for hours. Everyone thought he was sleeping. Then some kid poked him in the eye. I'll shoot you a text later on."

"Alright," I said. "Thanks, Tommy."

"Alright. I gotta go, buddy. Take care."

I put the phone down on the seat beside me and shifted. Snow was falling on the windshield. The flakes were thick and heavy. I was already invested in Malory Fleet but had another case to close first. It wasn't right but I decided to finish it fast and easy.

Dustin Colter worked at the industrial metal recycling facility down on the docks. His left foot was injured in an explosion and he'd been off work for about a month. Nobody was happy about it. I already had evidence that he could walk on the foot in question. Now, I just needed to seal the deal and close the case.

I knew that Dustin hung out at the Dooly's in Prince Edward Square. He used the VLTs. It was early in the day but he was off work so I decided to go down and check it out. It would be a stroke of luck but that's exactly what he went there looking for.

I parked in the lot in front of the Dollarama and went in through the doors. The place was a black hole during the day. Pop country played through broken speakers. The same girl as always was working. She had to fend off regulars with one hand and serve them drinks with the other.

"Hey, Lauren. How you doing?"

"Not bad. What'll you have?"

There were two men at the bar, ten feet apart, staring up at the row of screens. The Oilers were playing and losing. I ordered a pitcher and got a table in the back. As I walked to the corner, I scanned the room. Dustin wasn't there so I started to rack the balls. Lauren brought the pitcher over and set it down on the little round table in the corner. I used to come here with Madison sometimes—we'd shoot pool and drink 'til it closed, and then a little after.

There was a woman at the end of the bar around the corner. I hadn't noticed her at first. She was in her mid-forties and drinking red wine—a bad call in a place like this. She seemed comfortable, though, and it was early enough to assume that she'd only be there if she had the experience to know what she was doing.

The woman saw me looking at her. She eventually got down off the stool and walked across to the table with the wine glass in her hand. She was wearing jeans and a nice shirt. Her hair was well done. She had the sandpaper look of someone who made the most of the world and wasn't afraid of a little hurt. "Mind if I join you?" she asked.

I looked down at the racked balls and shook my head. "No problem," I said. "What do you play?"

"Eight-ball," she said. "Ball in hand."

"Dooly's rules?"

"Yeah," she said. She set down the wine glass and picked a cue from the rack.

"You want to break?"

"Sure," she said.

I took the triangle away and she set the cue ball behind the line, a little to the right. She broke hard and the balls scattered across the table and the cue ball spun to a stop in the middle. The ten dropped into a corner pocket.

She lined up another shot. I wanted to say something but didn't know what, so I just watched her play. She took a straight shot on the fifteen and put it in the side pocket. She hit the cue ball low and it stopped short. She was good, so I leaned back against the wall and took another drink. The song playing was bad. I didn't know it but I'd heard it a hundred times before.

*You never loved me like I loved you. You never loved me like I loved you.*

She sank the twelve in the far corner, cutting in at a 45-degree angle. The cue ball rolled with a gentle curve to the cushion and banked around the one. She potted the nine and eleven next. I leaned my cue against the wall. She wasn't calling pockets but the shots were obvious. She went around the table and leaned over, making a bridge with her thumb and index finger. She fired the cue ball hard, potting the fourteen in the side. The thirteen was easy. She dropped it with a gentle roll.

"Far corner," she said, pointing. The eight was lined up and she made the shot without effort, letting the cue ball slowly roll to the cushion.

"Thanks, hun," she said. She put the cue on the rack and picked up her wine and went back over to the bar. She climbed back up onto her stool and continued to drink, staring absently ahead. She was gone like that. I guess I just didn't give her a good enough game.

I racked again.

When I was eighteen, in Summerside, I got into a fight in a bar. I was too young to be in the place but they cared little about that there. Me and Tommy were splitting pitchers. Tommy's parents were from Cork. When he got a little drunk, he developed an accent, like a b'y from the rock. We were on our fourth pitcher in just as many hours. We were waiting to get a game of pool but kept missing our chance.

At a certain point, I went to the bathroom. When I came back, Tommy was trying to get the table from the local boys and things were getting heated. By the time I crossed the floor, one of the boys had his hands on Tommy.

Even with the beer, there was a moment of reflection. I remember making the decision to swing. Maybe the pause was imperceptible, overlooked by everyone else. To me, it's the moment that lasted the longest, a moment that remains. I realized that I could hit him and that I was going to do it. It could kill him but I was drunk enough to swing anyway. Everything telling me not to—conscience, consequence, convention—was set aside that easy.

The memory of the fight is fragmented, like a poorly buffered movie.

I threw the first punch. It caught him across the jaw and he looked up at me from the floor with wide eyes. His friend swung at Tommy, because Tommy was smaller, so I hit him too. I heard a crack and he sank. His crumpled body slumped on the floor still lingers in my mind.

I don't remember much after that, mostly yelling and shattering glasses, until we pushed through the front door and ran into the street.

When word filtered back to the academy, we were dressed down but not given up. It was a point of pride. They took care of their own. What surprised me then was how little I cared. I heard the crack and knew it meant nothing good for the guy who went down. But I didn't know who he was and never saw him again. Nothing surprises me anymore. This would be a tough job otherwise.

I sank all the balls in order. I was racking up again when Dustin Colter came in through the doors. Dustin was a scrawny guy. Tangled hair stuck out from beneath an old John Deere hat perched on his head, faded and blue. He wore a green plaid shirt and went right to the VLTs after ordering a beer. He sat hunched over on a stool feet away from the flickering yellow lights. His eyes glazed over and he was absorbed. I took a picture on my phone from across the room.

As I potted the next ball, the woman I'd played with stood up from the bar. I'd already missed one shot tonight and didn't want to miss another, so I walked up beside her. "So," I said. "You come here much?"

Her lips slipped into a small smirk. "Yeah," she said. "Why?"

I pointed to Dustin. "See that guy over there?"

"Yeah."

"He come in much?"

"I don't know," she said. "Why?"

"How often is he in here?"

"Few times a week, I guess. Why?" she repeated. This time, the *why* was more definite. I had to think fast.

"I'm with gambler's anonymous," I said. The moment the words left my lips, I regretted it. Her eyes were ice and she walked away from me just like that. She pushed open the front door, left this sanctuary, and re-entered the world. Again, I was in the black hole.

I went back to the table, finished my beer, and potted the occasional ball. When the pitcher was empty, I went back up to the bar with the rack and returned the balls. I discreetly took another picture of Dustin from the bar before Lauren came over. When she did, I paid for the table and left.

Red and blue lights swept the side of the building. A man was being loaded into the back of an ambulance on a stretcher. I could already tell that it would do him no good. They'll blame it on jib but the culprit was far larger than that. It was this city, this world.

I looked down past the industry offices and the food bank to the edge of the old loyalist burial ground. When I worked up north, a man had died in an accident. They loaded his body into a box and he disappeared in a plane. The landscape was unmarred. Nobody talked about him after that. I don't know why I remembered that then.

The sky was growing dark already. Dustin Colter was inside on the VLTs, healthy enough to lose all his money. I had what I needed to close the case. I'd leave it with Randy in the morning and move on.

My phone lit up. It was a message from Tommy: *"Det. Stuart Boucher."*

Nothing else.

The road was black and shiny from the rain. Heritage lamps reflected on the surface— small patches of amber, stretched and faded. The street was silent except for the hollow ring carrying through the evening from the harbour. Fog pulled down at the buildings. A church spire stretched up, black, in the distance, emerging alone from the cloud.

Muffled sounds slipped from the window of a pub. I made eye contact with a woman in the dim light through the glass. She brushed a strand of hair away from her eyes and turned back to her friends, laughing. The fog danced slowly down the row of brick buildings. When I opened the door, the air was thick and alive. Voices and speakers and glasses rushed past. I went to the bar. The other men watched me without making any effort to veil their interest. I ordered two beers and took them to a booth by the window. Music lingered somewhere beneath a symphony of voices.

Stuart Boucher came through the door and looked right to the booth by the window, where I was sitting. I nodded and he walked over. The light was low and artificial. He took a seat across from me and looked out the window. Snow was falling again. It would soon melt away.

Boucher was strongly built and had short, cropped hair that faded up from nothing to a flattop. He was a cop, through and through. He reached up and brushed snow from his head onto the booth beside him. He wiped more snow from the shoulders of his jacket.

"Thanks for meeting me," I said a little too quickly. The drinks I'd had at the pool hall had set me adrift.

"No problem." He picked up the Moosehead and took a long sip. "What do you need?"

"Like I said on the phone, I'm an investigator with Cormier."

"Yeah. What's this regarding?"

"I'm looking for Amanda Foster," I said. "I thought you might be able to help me out."

Boucher looked taken aback. "Amanda Foster? What do you want with her?"

"We want to find her. We've been hired for the job," I said.

"You don't want anything to do with that girl. Trust me."

"Why not?"

His jaw tightened. "She's fucking crazy," he said.

"What?"

"Who hired you? The mother?"

"Mother-in-law."

"Yeah," he said, nodding. "Malory. She's crazy too."

"What do you mean?"

"Look, I'm sorry but I can't help you out. Wish I could. Wish I knew where the girl was myself, trust me."

I looked around the bar. It was quiet. The only other people in the room were out of earshot. Far worse had probably been discussed in this bar anyway. "What do you mean by crazy?" I asked.

"Look, don't get me wrong, the son was a drug dealer, a scumbag. He isn't missed by many, but, if it was my son, I wouldn't want anything to do with that girl. And this lady can't seem to let her go. She's been in and out of the station for a year asking about her. Harassing cops at home. Harassing their wives. She's a mess."

I lifted my beer, drank from the bottle. "I don't really follow," I said. "What do you mean you wouldn't want anything to do with Amanda if Jason was your son?"

Boucher looked at me closely, sussing me out. Maybe he just knew I was drunk. "I guess it doesn't matter anymore," he said, "and I don't really give a fuck, anyway." He paused. "She killed her son." His eyes were hard and steady.

I stared across the table over the bottles. "Malory killed Jason?"

Boucher shook his head. "No," he said. "I mean the girl killed Malory's son. Amanda killed Jason." He paused. "Everyone fucking knows it, including Malory." He glanced around the bar. There was no one in earshot. "They're both crazy."

"Why wasn't she charged?"

"Trust me, we tried. It's almost impossible to convict a woman."

This sounded like something from another time but I decided to let it sit. Fighting him on that front didn't seem like it would do me any favours. "Why do you think Amanda did it?"

Boucher shook his head. "I can't get into this," he said. "My advice? Drop the case. Stay the fuck away from Malory. If you find Amanda, call me. She's getting away with murder." He reached into his pocket and took out a business card. He finished the beer and left the bottle beside the card. "Thanks for the beer," he said. "I gotta get back to work."

I stayed sitting there by the window as Boucher walked back up to his car. He got in, started the engine, and pulled out onto the road.

I wondered if it was true. I wondered if Malory was crazy and if Amanda really could've shot her boyfriend outside their apartment that Halloween. I put on my coat and walked to the door too. It was cold. Zipping the coat up to the collar, I walked back up the block with my hands in my pockets. At Princess Street I unlocked the minivan parked along the curb in front of the office. I opened the side door and took out a folder that was lying on the seat inside. The stairs up to the office creaked beneath my weight. Low lights flickered. Inside, I turned on the light and sat at the desk in the corner. I began to look through the folder. It was background information—what little I had already been able to gather about Amanda Foster.

Amanda grew up near Moncton and moved to Saint John a couple of years before she disappeared. She played volleyball in high school. There was a picture of her in the file. She was sitting on a bench by the water looking directly at the photographer, something steady in her eyes. She didn't look crazy.

After moving to Saint John, she worked in a cycle of restaurants uptown. She made friends. I had a few names. That was where the trail ran cold. Even her parents didn't seem to exist. I went into the bathroom and drank a glass of water and washed my mouth, then went out, down the block and cut through the park.

At the corner, two cops were pushing a teenager into the back of a cruiser. There was a can of bear spray on the roof. He was pleading: "I swear on my life, I didn't know."

I went down the hill towards the water and up along the road to the harbourfront. The patios were empty and the tables were stacked up beneath fresh snow. There was a woman leaning against the banister a little further down, smoking. I thought her eyes were on me. I'm not a good-looking guy but I some-times think I've got the kind of face a woman likes if she doesn't like herself all that much.

Snippets of conversation slipped from the fog: *"So she says to me, she says, Tommy was drinkin' some heavy..." "Oh, I tell ya..."*

I went up through the patio to the door of the first restaurant and opened it. Air was blowing hot through a vent above the door. The restaurant was empty except for a young woman tidying up near the back and a bald man standing behind the counter watching her. They both turned to look at me.

"Can I help you?" the man asked.

"I just have a few questions," I said, walking towards the counter. "I'm looking for the manager."

"I'm the owner."

"Even better."

"How can I help you?"

"I'm an investigator with the Cormier Agency."

"The what?"

"Cormier Agency," I repeated. "I'm a private investigator."

"A private detective?"

"More or less," I said. I leaned on the counter. "We're working a missing persons case." The man's face shifted. "We're looking for a woman who used to work here."

"Amanda Foster," he said.

"That's right."

The owner shook his head. "I told the police a hundred times. I haven't seen her."

"They've been in?"

"A bunch of times. Not for a while now," he said. "One used to come around a lot."

"Stuart Boucher?"

The owner nodded. "Boucher, yeah. He was real thorough. I'll tell you what I told him.

She worked here for a few months. Nice girl. Partied too much. One day she didn't show up for work and that's all I know."

"You have no idea where she went?"

"No," the man said. "I don't mean to be rude but I've been through this over and over. I'm sorry for her family but there's not really anything I can do to help you out."

"Was she friendly with any of the girls here?" I asked.

"A couple."

"Mind if I talk to some?"

The owner looked over at the girl in the corner. "Ashley!" he called. She turned. "Come over here. This man has a few questions for you," he said. He held up his hand and spread his fingers. "Five minutes," he mouthed.

The girl was in her early twenties. Small, slim, and dyed blonde hair tied back in a ponytail. She came over and set a cloth down on the counter. "Yeah?"

"You knew Amanda Foster?" I asked.

She glanced at the owner. "Yeah," she said. "Why?"

"We're looking for her. Missing persons case."

"You a cop?"

"Private investigator."

"That's a real job?"

"It is."

"What do you want to know?"

"When was the last time you saw her?"

"Like a year ago," she said. "Just before she went missing?"

"At work?"

"At a party," she said. "Some of the girls went out and we met up with her at a party in the South End."

"How did she seem?"

"Normal," the girl said. "I don't know. I didn't notice anything weird if that's what you mean."

"How long before she disappeared was that?"

"A week, maybe?"

"Did you know her boyfriend?"

"Jason?" she shook her head. "No. I met her after all of that. She was going through a tough time." She glanced over at the owner. "It didn't help that the cops wouldn't leave her alone," she added. "She couldn't move on."

"Alright, back to work," the owner said uneasily.

"One last thing. Whose party was it?"

"I don't know," she said. "A friend of a friend, I think." She paused. "If you're looking for her, I'd talk to this girl, Emma. She lived with her for a while after... all that stuff happened. I think they were pretty close."

"Ok, thanks," I said.

"Got what you need?" the owner asked.

"Yeah," I said. "Thanks."

I left and walked along the harbourfront, leaned on the railing and looked out to the water. The clouds were low. Ice was piling up along the edge of the murky water. The curve of shadow from the clouds was nearly blue.

I thought about the details of life that would slip in and out of perception so briefly, only to be noticed later, things forgotten then reinvented. I was thinking about Madison and the way she'd meet my eyes. The city wasn't the same after she left me. I found myself, now and then, going to the places we used to go. Sometimes, I went to her apartment to keep an eye on her and the cars that came and went.

I pulled out my phone and made a call. It rang twice.

"Hello?"

"Malory?"

"Yes?"

"It's Frank. From the Cormier Agency," I said.

"Hey, Frank," she said.

I looked down at the grey water beneath. "I've got some more questions for you," I said. "If you've got time."

"When?"

"Whenever."

"How's now?"

I looked at my watch. "I can be there in fifteen minutes."

When she agreed, I walked back up to Princess. I was still a little drunk but it wasn't far to go. I started the engine on the second attempt and pulled out onto the street, following the one-way streets back around to Union and then over to the North End, looking down at the grid of rail lines leading to the dockyards.

Saint John wasn't a company town but it may as well have been. In Saint John, there was a company and it owned the town. It owned oil and lumber, railways, shipping, and trucking. It owned gas stations and hardware stores. It owned shipbuilding and construction. It owned the only newspaper and most of the radio stations. More importantly, it owned the land.

When I moved here, I thought it was unlike any place I'd known before. A billion-dollar empire: oil, gas, and lumber. Children lived in squalor: mold, mice, and methamphetamine. Malnourishment and impoverishment fed the appetites of the wealthy. No grocery stores in the heart but uptown galleries hawked cheap art at high prices, pandering to parasites.

I've since learned that every city is the same. Some just hide it better than others.

We sat in the living room at the front of the apartment. It smelled like cigarettes and a litterbox. There was a white cat named Casper clawing at the edge of the couch when I came in. Malory shooed it away. Framed pictures of Jason and Amanda hung on the walls. There was a picture of them together and I couldn't help but think of Madison. I was jealous for a moment and then I remembered that he was dead and she was missing. What I really wanted, more than anything, was to have Madison back. Since that was not possible, I wanted no one to have her.

Beneath the picture of them, there was one of Jason at about twelve years old holding a 20-inch fish in his hands. We were never big into fishing. It reminded my mom too much of my dad. But she wanted me to have the experience, and I was the same age as Jason was in that picture. We left early. I don't know what time but it was before the sun came up and the air was still. The putter of the motor melted into the lake. We sat and sucked on leeches as the morning eased into day. We cast and I soon caught a 26-incher. He called me a natural. He took a picture of me holding the fish, then slipped the trophy back into the lake. I pulled two more before I got one we could keep. We took the hook out and put the catch in a bucket of water. We went to a little island that he knew and I jumped out to guide the craft along the shore. I tied up to a tree and he showed me how to kill the fish with the back of the blade—a single blow, clean and painless. I cut a slit millimetres from the tail and slid the knife along the side to take as much meat as possible from the catch. We threw bones, guts, and the head to waiting gulls so nothing went to waste.

"You can sit anywhere," Malory said. I looked away from the picture, torn. She sat down beside an ashtray and lit a smoke. I sat on the soft, ragged sofa across from her with my back to the window. I could feel the cold air coming through it.

"I talked to a girl who worked with Amanda," I said. It seemed like the best place to start. The main course would come later. "She saw her at a party just before she went missing. A week or so. She said that I should talk to a girl named Emma."

Malory nodded. "Emma, yeah. She moved in with Amanda for a few months after Jason's death."

"Do you know what her last name is?"

"McLoughlin."

"Were they close?"

"Pretty good friends," Malory said. "Emma was good to her, kind."

"She still around?"

"Yeah," Malory said, tapping the cigarette over the ashtray. "But they stopped living together about a month before Amanda went missing. Emma moved in with her boyfriend."

"Know how to find her?"

"She works at Service New Brunswick. I see her there sometimes."

I made a note. "Thanks." I looked at a picture of Amanda on the wall above the couch. She was in a bathing suit on a beach, Mispec, maybe. "Can you tell me a bit about Amanda?" I asked. "It might help the case."

Malory followed my eyes. "What do you want to know?"

"Whatever you want to tell me."

"Jason met her at a party in the South End," Malory said. "She was a saving grace."

"What do you mean by that?" I asked.

"He was on a dark road before that. She was able to keep up and keep him interested but didn't have that self-destructive streak that seems to plague the rest of the generation."

"When did you first meet her?"

"Jason brought Amanda around about a week after they first met." Malory tapped the cigarette. She smiled a little. "It was like we'd known one another for years. She just fit. I knew right away that she was the one for him."

"You talked about her before as a daughter."

"She was, basically," Malory said. "She didn't have much in the way of family. Her mom died when she was a baby and her dad was never around. He moved to South Africa or somewhere like that. We spent a lot of time together, even when Jason wasn't around."

"How long did you know her?"

"About two years when Jason died." She stubbed out the cigarette and looked at me. "There's a little bit of him in her," she said. "That's why it's so hard. When she was around, it didn't feel like he was completely gone. He lived on, in a way. Now, it's like..." she trailed off.

I nodded and let the cat lick my hand. "Can I ask you a few questions about him?" I asked.

"What do you want to know?"

"He was born here in Saint John?"

Malory nodded. "Yeah."

"You were living here, then?"

"I've always lived here," she said. "Born and raised."

"And his dad?"

"He didn't know him."

I hesitated. "This might be a little sensitive but I guess you've been through it all before. Jason was a dealer?"

"Jason was involved in some of that," she said. I waited. She lit another cigarette and then sank back into the seat, looking at me through pinched eyes. "He sold drugs, yes."

"That's what you meant about him heading down a dark road?"

"He was getting arrested. He got in fights. He didn't take care of himself."

"Do you know when that all started?"

"When he was a kid, I guess. High school. He got in with a crowd, you know how it is. It's the same story over and over."

"I spoke with the detective on Jason's case," I said. It was what I'd been wanting to say all night. Boucher had a different story than her.

Malory sat up straight. There was something in her eyes—anger or fear. "Why?"

"I need all the information I can get."

"What did he say? That I was crazy?"

"Yeah," I nodded. "He did."

Malory shook her head. "He's the crazy one," she said.

"What do you mean?"

"I told you not to talk to the cops," she said. "They don't give a fuck about helping. I've been down that road."

"What do you mean he's crazy?"

"He's a woman beater," she said. "He's got two domestics."

"Really?"

"Yeah. And those are just the ones they arrested him for."

"He said you were harassing cops at their houses."

Malory laughed. It was bitter. "I was try-ing to get them to do their fucking job." She looked past me at the pictures on the wall. "Did he try to tell you that Amanda killed Jason too?"

I nodded again. She really had been down this road before.

She shook her head. "What a piece of shit. He's the crazy one. He got it in his head that Amanda killed Jason and wouldn't let it go. Wouldn't look at anything else. Of course, there was nothing there so they couldn't press any charges. They ran into a dead end."

"Amanda was their main suspect?"

"She was their only suspect."

I shifted position, leaning forward on the soft couch. "Do you think that there is any possibility...?"

Malory shook her head. "No. None."

A dark cloud passed. It was out of my mouth before I could stop and think it through. "Do you think that this has anything to do with her disappearance?"

Malory looked directly into my eyes. For the first time, I felt that I understood her. I knew why she had come to us—and I wished that she hadn't. "Yes," she said. "I do."

There was a weight on my chest suddenly. I swallowed, clearing my throat. "You think that Detective Boucher has something to do with her disappearance."

"Maybe," she said.

The room was silent other than the sound of the cat pulling at the back of the sofa. "Do you think that Amanda is still alive, Malory?"

"All I know is that she's missing," Malory said, "and that I want to find her. I want to know what happened."

"You told me that you thought she was still alive last time we spoke."

"I think I'd feel it if she wasn't. I feel the void with Jason. With Amanda, it isn't the same. I don't know what I think. Where could she have gone?"

I looked at her and wondered if she was saying what I thought she was. I wasn't even willing to voice the question so I asked another one instead. "Who do you think killed your son?"

"I don't know."

"Don't you think that finding the real killers would clear Amanda's name, at least?"

Malory stubbed out the cigarette and reached down to pet the cat at her feet. When she was done, she lit another smoke. "It's no use," she said. "I've been there. I've tried that."

"These cases can take years."

"Do you know what percent of murders are solved?"

The stale cloud was growing dense. "I don't."

"Fifty percent."

"That's low," I said.

She drew on the cigarette. "You have to think—most of those are probably the easy ones. The killer is on the scene, wife killers, ones in public with witnesses, heat of the moment things. Then you also have to figure that in a lot of the cases they actually got the wrong guy, so the real number's even less."

"So, what are you saying?" I asked.

She looked past me to the framed photos on the wall. "I'm saying that I'm done with that," she said, shaking her head. "But there's still some hope for Amanda, and I want some answers."

PART II

Malory's son was dead and her daughter in law was missing. For all I knew, she was dead too. I wasn't feeling good any longer. The fact that this case was real was starting to hit me. Malory was not a broken woman but there was something broken in her. She was a survivor but survival was taking its toll.

I parked uptown and walked to a bar near the water. It was dark and quiet and the only other people who went there didn't want to be seen. I kept thinking about the things that mattered in life. When I did that, all I landed on was Madison. We used to drive down to Saints Rest Marsh and walk the trails. The marsh ran into the cove. Where it ended, the ocean began. There were blue herons, bald eagles, and cormorants. Once, a whale carcass rose from the depths as we stood and stared out across the vast expanse, searching for seals among the silver ridges.

I remembered foliage and fern, moss and stone, and a mist so thick it hung between us—the slow wash of waves on the shore and the distant bellows of an iron whale at sea. Madison was against the tree in the damp bark smell and nothing could stop it from being right. When it's wet after rain, the pores of the earth open up and the whole world begins to breathe. And though there were the sounds of the birds and the leaves and the insects around us, it was silent, and what I mean by that is that there was nobody else but us.

I knew that I'd messed it all up and that there was no going back. If you're lucky in this world, you probably only get one real shot at doing it right and I'd wasted mine. What I had left were a lot of long years and a feeling in my chest like I was missing a lung. I kept thinking about Boucher, too, and wondering if it was actually possible that he had something to do with Amanda's disappearance.

I was sitting there at the bar with a beer in my hand, feeling a lot, when the door opened and a woman walked in. She was familiar but it took a moment to place her. Her name was Hannah and she was a girl I'd known for a brief time in Summerside. She walked up to the bar and took a seat. I could tell she was trying to avoid my gaze because she'd come there to be alone and I was a man alone at a bar, and nothing good ever came from that.

Hannah had dark hair and her eyes were dark too. She used to hang out at a bar off Water Street with her friends. On a couple of nights, we left the bar with a few people and sat down at the boardwalk looking out over the ocean at the stars, passing around a mickey. One night when it was warm, we went down onto the beach and stripped out of our clothes and dove into the ocean, drunk and laughing. I felt alive. The taste of salt and rye, the fresh island air against my face, the cold water sending tremors through my body.

I can still remember how she looked coming out shivering and glistening beneath the stars, red sand clinging desperately to her skin. Right then, she and the world around us was breathtaking. Maybe to everyone else it was just another night but, to me, it felt good to be with people who did things like that. Prince Edward Island was a desolate place. I was perpetually homesick. Being on that beach was a moment of sanctuary, an oasis. It meant a lot.

I tried to catch her eye but she wouldn't have it, so I got down off the stool and stood there for a moment. Eventually she looked over. "It's Hannah, right?"

She looked me up and down with distrust. I knew what she was scared of but I've never really been a man who knew what to do with simple lust. Instead, I fall in headfirst and don't emerge until I've drowned.

"Yeah," she said. "Do I know you?"

"Frank Cain," I said. "We met in Summerside," I said. "A while ago now."

She looked at me and squinted. "Oh, yeah," she finally said. I couldn't tell if she made the connection. I knew that when she remembered, she'd be glad to see me.

"I just thought I should say hello. It's been a long time."

"It has," she said.

"Mind if I sit down?"

She hesitated. "Free country."

I sat down on the stool beside her and took another drink. She was fun back then and I used to look at her a lot before we ever got around to speaking. She was one of those girls you saw smiling from a distance and just knew you had to meet. There was something in the smile. It made you feel at home. Madison had a smile like that.

"What brings you to Saint John?" I asked. I tended to think in transient terms.

"I've got family here," Hannah said. "You from Saint John?"

"No," I said. "New Glasgow, remember?"

"Oh yeah," she said. "Guess I forgot."

"You're from O'Leary, right?"

"How'd you know that?" she asked.

"You told me."

"Right."

The TV above the bar was playing silent commentary from the game. "You grew up in Summerside though, right?"

She looked at me closely. "Yeah, basically. What were you doing there, again?"

"I was at the Police Academy," I said.

She nodded then. "Oh, right."

"So, what are you doing in Saint John, then?"

"Family." She looked down at the counter for a moment before she spoke again. "Sorry, but did we know each other well?" she asked. "I can't remember."

I thought about it for a while. The condensation on the outside of the bottle drenched the label and I picked at it. There was a music in the background. It was a pop song, upbeat and crooning with heartache. "Not really," I said, eventually.

She nodded. "I didn't think so."

We sat there for a while drinking our beer and eventually I got down off the stool and said goodbye. I must've known her better than she knew me. She was a distant memory that had hardened and become something it wasn't. That was something I was beginning to know a lot about. I stepped outside to the cackle of the gulls that, like a violin out of tune, carried down from the rooftops along the water.

Madison stood in the window looking out at the dark street. The view was at the back of the building and did not look down over the park. The curtains hung open and her silhouette was trapped against the light.

I wished that I could tell her about Amanda and ask her what she thought. It was early and the grass was wet with dew. I leaned against the short stone wall and looked up. In the dim morning light, beneath the cover of fog, I was safe from her gaze. She turned and went away from the window and I was left staring up at the brick wall.

The streetlights cast their glow across the haze and the sun was beginning to rise over the harbour below. Headlights were shaking up the road. I stepped back. A grey car passed by and stopped at the corner. The windows were tinted black.

Leaning back against the wall, I saw the light in the window above turn off. A minute later, Madison came around the front of the building and hurried to the passenger side of the waiting vehicle. She opened the door and got in. There was a mutual laugh before the door clapped. The car's brake lights faded and it sped through the intersection and disappeared around the corner.

I walked up Sydney and cut through the old burial ground to the Tim Hortons. Crumbling gravestones sank into the grass. A line of cars waited at the drive-thru but inside it was quiet. I bought a coffee and a muffin and sat beside a window to watch the cars and people pass. An overflowing shopping cart rattled over the cracked sidewalk. A woman drew her hands into her sleeves and stepped off the curb, straying into the road. She returned to the curb and sat down with her head in her arms, shaking, and then stood and went back into the road in a panic. I could see it was a habit, a pattern.

When I finished the muffin, I went back out. The air was misty and light. Breathing deep, the pungent smell of rotting food and decay filled my lungs. A man slumped beside the door looked up. "Got a smoke, bud?"

"Sorry, man."

There were a few old buckets in the lot, mostly battered Pontiacs and Chryslers, and the asphalt was crumbling. I checked the time, sipped the coffee, and started towards the office. Steam rose through the mist, carrying its burnt aroma.

For some reason, I kept thinking about that picture of Jason and the salmon. I only went one other time that I can remember. A couple of years after I went with my mom, I went fishing with a friend in the country. He was the type of guy I looked up to. The type of guy who wasn't scared of anything. Or, maybe he was just scared of everything and had built up a hard shell around himself. He led us down a dirt road and pushed through the bushes to the shore. We brought a rod and nothing else but the shaft of a broken golf club that I found in a ditch along the way. He cast into the lake and the line trailed, bobbing. After a few minutes, it jerked. He started to reel right away. I didn't know much about fishing but I knew then that he didn't either.

He continued to reel and I said nothing. It was a good thing because soon he was fighting. Somehow, the fish was hooked. He pulled and the dorsal fin cut through the face of the lake. He pulled hard and the fish broke the surface, the sunlight screaming in its scales. It slapped down a few feet closer to shore. His smile grew. He reeled faster after that. The fish tore towards the shore, skidding and bouncing across the glassy water. Its cheek should have torn but somehow it managed to hold. The next thing I knew the rod was bent and the fish was dangling above the rocks. He grabbed the line, dropped the rod, and raised the catch in triumph. For a moment I stood with him, grinning.

Then the animal thrashed back. It whipped from side to side, fighting the hook, ripping its own cheek apart. It was a futile struggle. Even if it had managed to break free it would have fallen to the rocks below. As soon as it started to fight back, I saw the fear in his eyes. He held it far away as he could and screeched at me to hit it. I looked down at the broken golf club and realized that it would actually be used. I still remember the weight of the club in my palm. I remember the spinning line and the bulging eyes. I stepped up and swung the headless shaft like a baseball bat. I felt the dull thud of contact and the shock in my wrists. The fish sailed through the air, bounced from a tree, and landed on the rocks. My friend swore and dropped to his knees. He pulled the embedded hook from his hand. Flapping on the rock, the fish's eyes protruded from its head, popped from one of the impacts, and a dent cut into its back. Its mouth slowly opened and closed. Its gills did the same. Occasionally it twitched.

My friend picked up the club, walked over to where it lay, and began slamming it down hard. Goo and flesh oozed from the sockets to the gaping mouth. The shaft bent with every blow. Each landed awkwardly, leaving the fish alive. The air was humid and warm. Thuds carried over the lake until he stopped swinging. He wasn't laughing when he tossed the battered fish back into the water and threw the bent shaft into the trees. Blood ran down his chin as he sucked on the cut on his palm. The fish sank below the surface, drifting from view. I knew it would twitch a few more times on the way down and then re-emerge somewhere else when the gasses started to build.

"Jesus Christ. What the hell have we gotten ourselves into?"

"I know, Randy."

"So, the cops think that Amanda killed Jason and the mother thinks that the cops killed Amanda?"

"She didn't say that. She still thinks Amanda might be alive," I said. "She does think the cop, the detective, might have something to do with the disappearance."

"And all of them think that everybody else is crazy."

"Yeah," I said.

Randy leaned back in the chair and tapped the pen on the desk. The end had been chewed to pieces. Light was streaming in through the narrow windows along the wall. Snowflakes were drifting down, casting small shadows. The rooftops across the road were flat. "I think we should drop the case," he said. "This is too much."

"I don't think we should, Randy. I think we should see it through. A little further at least. I get the sense that Malory and Amanda weren't as close as Malory thinks. There's just something about the way she tells the story that doesn't quite make sense. I want to dig into that a little too."

Randy looked down at the file and tapped his pen some more. "I can't afford to get on the wrong side of the police department," he said. "This business is tough enough as it is."

"It's a missing persons case," I said. "We just need to treat it that way."

He looked tired. There were bags under his eyes. "Well, what's your next step?" he asked.

"Talk to a couple of friends," I said. "There's one, Emma, an old roommate, who keeps coming up."

"You know where to find her?"

"I think so.

"Ok," Randy said. "Be careful. And report back to me every step of the way. Don't fuck this up, Frank."

"I won't." I stood up and left the office.

The sky was grey—lighter where the sun was rising. It was a cold morning and the air struggling through the vents smelled like dust.

Service New Brunswick ran government hours so it wouldn't be possible to get Emma during the day. I drove to Waterloo Village to see another friend instead, Melanie, but I didn't know if I'd get anything from her. I'd come across her name on social media and the address was easy to find. I was casting a wide net to see what came in. Sometimes, that's the way the job's done.

Melanie was coming out the front of the apartment building when I pulled up across the street. She was pushing a baby in a stroller. It felt like the wrong topic to bring up in front of a child but I was already there, so I opened the door of the van and got out. I glanced up and down, then crossed the road. "Melanie?"

She was wrestling the stroller through the doorway onto the uneven sidewalk. "Yeah?" she asked.

"My name's Frank," I said. "I'm an investigator. Is it alright if I ask you a few questions?"

She leaned on the handles. "What's this about?" she asked. She looked uncomfortable already.

"Amanda Foster," I said. "You knew her, right?"

"I don't think I can really help you out."

"Why's that?"

"I didn't know her that well. I saw her around. We went to the same parties."

"Just a couple questions. It won't take long at all," I said. I buried my hands in my pockets. It was cold. A man down the block began to yell and we both glanced his way.

"What do you want to know?" she asked.

"What did you know about her?"

"Like I said, not much. She was really nice."

"What else?"

She paused, glancing down at the stroller. "She was one of those girls that guys would fall in love with, you know? They didn't just want to take her to bed."

"Why do you say that?"

"It's just the way it was." The baby started to cry and she stooped down beside it, shushing it. She looked up at me. "You wouldn't want her around your boyfriend," she said. "Not because she was like that, or anything, just because they'd pay a little too much attention to her."

"Why do you think that?"

"It's just the way it was." She was fumbling with a pacifier for the baby. "You've seen the pictures, she was pretty. But, it was more than that. It was a personality thing. She was bubbly. She was kind of... I don't know, ditzy but smart, you know? I can't explain it. She was just one of those girls."

"You keep saying *was*," I said.

"Yeah."

"You don't think she's around anymore."

"No," Melanie said, her face without expression.

"Why not."

"People don't disappear without a trace," she said. "Not anymore. Not if they're still alive."

"Do you have any idea what happened?"

Melanie shook her head. "No," she said, standing back up. The way she said it, I believed her. She didn't know and I don't think she wanted to know.

"Who would you talk to if you wanted to find out?"

"I don't know. Maybe Mrs. Fleet."

"Jason's mother?"

"Yeah."

"Anybody else?"

"Not really. I wouldn't go asking around though, to be honest." She paused again, looking past me. "She had an ex I kind of knew. A guy named Alex. It wasn't serious."

"Do you know his last name?"

"Brewer. I only know they dated because he was kind of a family friend when I was younger."

"Was he in the same crowd?"

"He wasn't like Jason, if that's what you're asking. He was more of... like a hipster kind of guy."

"Do you know where I could find him?"

"No," she said. "I haven't seen him in years." She checked the time on her phone. "Look, I really need to..."

"Yeah," I said. "Thanks. Go on. Thanks for your help."

She gave me a weak smile and headed down the slush-covered sidewalk, pushing the stroller ahead of her. After a few steps she turned and looked back. "Go see his mom," she called. "Alex's. Sharon Brewer. She lives on the West End. You can always get to a man through his mother."

"Thanks," I said.

I checked my watch. I didn't know if it would lead me anywhere but I had the time to find out, so I got back into the van and pulled out my phone. It didn't take me long to find an address for Sharon Brewer. It never does with the older crowd.

I took the minivan and drove across to the west side. Over there, you got the worst of the smell but the houses were big and the views were good. Hers was further than I expected, nearly out of city bounds. It sat on a ridge overlooking the lower land and the ocean behind it. I parked in the driveway behind a magenta Buick that looked like it hadn't moved in a decade.

I wasn't sure if anyone was home because all the windows were dark and a lot of the curtains were drawn. The door was painted white but it was a bad job. I could see the grey streaks of something beneath.

I knocked and waited. I was about to leave when I heard the creak of floorboards inside. A moment later, the door unlocked and began to open slightly. An aged woman stood warily in the shadows of the house. She peered out through the crack and didn't bother, or dare, to say hello.

"Mrs. Brewer?" I asked.

"Depends who's asking."

"I'm Frank Cain," I said.

Her eyes peered out beneath a hooded brow. I could barely see them for the shadows.

"I'm looking for Alex," I added.

"You won't find him here," she said in a cold and sharp voice.

"When was the last time you saw him?" I could smell her from where I stood. Like onions and mildew. I wondered if it was her clothes or her skin.

She shook her head. "I can't remember."

"Any idea where I might find him?"

"My knees are shot," she said. "Come inside."

It was such an instant shift that, had she not led the way so quickly, I might not have followed. There was something unsettling about it all. I stepped through the doorway into the musk. The lights were off and it was dark inside. She disappeared through a doorway to the right and I followed.

The front room was off the entryway. It was nearly empty. Its large windows looked out to the sea, but somehow seemed to give no light. Outside, the air felt open and alive—clean. Within these walls, it was something else entirely. The room smelled like musty wood. The walls were oak and the floors were ash. Heat hung heavy between them. She sank into a faded armchair in the corner with the wide window behind her. She was looking in, facing away from the world.

A brown moth fluttered with the ashes in an old wood stove in the corner. I wondered when it had gotten in and if it would get back out. The moth landed on the glass and stopped, then lifted its wings again and disappeared into the shadows of the charred walls at the back of the stove.

"So, you haven't seen Alex in a while?" I asked.

"No," she said. "He moved to Montreal about three years ago."

"Does he ever come back to visit?" I asked.

"Christmas," she said, "the holidays."

"Has he been in touch with Amanda Foster, at all?"

"Not that I know of," she said. The woman leaned forward in her seat. "Is that what this is about?" she asked. "Amanda?"

"Yes," I said. "I'm trying to find her."

"Good luck," she said. She was sitting with her purple legs splayed wide. The thin fabric of her housecoat draped over her bony knees like a gentle caress.

"What do you mean?" I asked.

"No one else has been able to." She shook her head, sinking back into the cushion. "A horrible thing."

"Does Alex ever talk about her?"

"Not really. They weren't together for long. They were a bad match." She looked at me closely. Her eyes were blue. Stunning. I hadn't noticed before.

"I think she knew something that someone didn't want her to," she said. Her eyes suddenly flashed like a storm at sea, with dark thoughts swimming beneath the surface. Behind her, I could see the sky. The moon was nearly orange and the sky grey behind it. We were close enough to see the smokestacks but they seemed a world away. I had a hard time believing that she could really know anything about what went on in the heart of the city from out here.

"You think she knew who killed Jason." I had little time for performance or intrigue.

She nodded slowly. Her expression was sombre, grave. "Yes."

"Why do you say so?"

"Why else would they kill her," she asked, "a girl like that?"

I stared at her for a little while and swallowed. When I did, it felt like I'd taken something toxic from the air, something that burned at the back of my throat. I wiped my hand across my brow, slick with salt. The entire situation was unsettling. "I'd better go," I said. "I have an appointment."

"I didn't ask you to stay."

I reached into my pocket and drew out my wallet.

"I don't need your charity," she said.

"I just wanted to give you my card," I said, "in case Alex calls."

"He won't."

I set the card down on the first clear surface I saw, the arm of an old rocking chair beside me. It was an odd place to put it. It rested awkwardly. "Thanks for your time," I said.

"What else do I have?"

I was sitting in the minivan down the block, thinking about the fact that nothing was adding up, when I saw a black car I recognized at the intersection beside our office on Princess. Stuart Boucher was in the front seat. He was lingering in the way that cops do, looking for trouble. I watched him head down the block. I wondered what he was doing out front, peering in at the office. Another car coming up the road slowed behind him. With the pressure, he rolled through.

I shifted gears and pulled out onto the road behind, following with the safety of the second car between us. I didn't really know what I was doing but Malory had her suspicions about him and now I did too. There was just something about Boucher that made me think something was off about him. I wanted to call Tommy to learn what I could about him but I knew that the best way to lose my in at the station was to try to use him against another cop. They looked out for their own.

Boucher was going up King towards the park. As he turned at the intersection, the side of his face was visible. It was cold in the shadows. He glanced past me and I felt ice along my spine.

The car in front of me pulled through but I stayed at the intersection across from the park, watching. I was suddenly uncertain about going any further. Fucking with a cop was a good way to ruin your life.

He continued moving towards the city market, passing the Service New Brunswick office. I thought about Emma. That was a solid lead and I couldn't afford to get distracted. A car behind me honked. I quickly pulled through and turned left.

I'd decided to dive back into an old clue I'd allowed to slip away, so was waiting outside the SNB office as men smoked and talked by the bus stop. There were more faded tattoos per square foot in uptown Saint John than anywhere else on Earth. And there was an unwritten law that you couldn't follow any trend newer than five years—thirteen was the sweet spot.

Uptown Saint John would have been downtown anywhere else. It was where all the local businesses were, where the streets were busy. It was called uptown because Saint John was a port city and the ships came in at the harbour, which was physically lower. Crews walked "up" to the centre of the city. Here, huddled shapes rested on the benches in the park across the road, bundled for warmth. The wind carried a damp cold that sank and stayed. The smell of weed was in the air like a humid botanical garden.

At 4:45, workers started coming out of the office, heading around the side to the car park. I waited for the face of the woman to appear. I'd found her on Instagram. In some ways, the job had never been easier. At 4:57, she came out the front door. She was walking alone.

"Emma," I said.

She turned to look at me. "Yes?"

"I'm Frank Cain. I'm a private investigator."

Emma looked me up and down, uncertainty in her eyes. She was wearing business clothes beneath a black and white winter coat, and held on to a travel mug and a purse. She looked tired.

"We're working a missing persons case," I added.

Emma shook her head. Her face was pale. Her green eyes avoided mine. "I'm sorry," she said. "I don't have time for this."

"I can meet at a better time," I said. "Whenever works for you."

"I'm very busy," she said.

"Any time. Evenings, weekends, whenever."

Emma turned away. "I'm sorry," she said. "I have to go."

She was nearly shaking. She knew something, I thought. "Please," I said, stepping forward. "Malory already lost a son. Even if you don't think you know anything, you might be able to help."

"I've talked to the police. I've talked to Malory. It's time to let this go."

"It's not that easy."

Emma turned back to look at me. She glanced over her shoulder quickly. "Leave it alone," she said. "I don't know anything. I'm sorry for Malory but Amanda isn't her daughter."

"She's close to her."

"Not as close as she thinks," she said.

"What does that mean?"

"Jason's death was hard on her but she can't replace him with Amanda."

"You know them well?"

"I know Amanda well. I knew Jason, too. Listen, Malory didn't know either as well as she thought." She glanced over her shoulder again. "I have to get going."

"Malory's going t–"

"Tell Malory to drop it," Emma said, agitated. "Amanda doesn't want to be found." Her face melted as soon as she spoke.

The realization shook me so hard that I reached out, whether to simply touch her shoulder or balance myself, I don't know. "You know where she is."

"I have to go," she said. She hurried to the parking lot without looking back.

I stood in the middle of the sidewalk in front of the government building. A bus rolled to a stop beside me. I went down to the end of the block and crossed the street, cut through the old burial grounds, and walked back to the office, all the while my legs trembling.

"She knows where Amanda is," I said, planting myself down across from Randy.

The heater had been on for some time and the room was pretty warm. I could hear it rattling. I unzipped my coat and hung it over the back of the chair. This was the break that had been skirting us since we started. This was our *in*.

"So, she's alive?"

"Looks that way," I said. "Emma, this friend, said she doesn't want to be found. Asked us to tell Malory to stop looking."

"That so?"

"It is."

Randy lifted the pen to his mouth and chewed the end, his teeth peeking out beneath his parting lips. He leaned back, thinking hard. "Think we should tell Malory?"

"That the girl is alive?"

"And the rest."

I'm not exactly sure why but I'd been asking myself the same thing. I was growing wary of Malory. "It's her case," I said. "Her money."

Randy pulled the pen out of his mouth and pointed the gnarled end at me. "So, this girl, the friend, knows where to find her?"

"Seems that way."

"See if you can find out," Randy said.

"She doesn't want to talk," I said.

"They never do."

"Want me to surveil her?"

Randy nodded.

"What about Malory?"

"Wait a little longer," he said. "Let's see where this goes. Speculation isn't worth much in any case."

It was my turn to nod.

"You need cash?" he asked.

"I'll keep my receipts." I took my coat and went out the door, down to the minivan parked on the street below. I got in and turned the key, letting the van warm up.

The house was square and white. A missing step on the porch led to white doors. The numbers beside the door were missing too but you could read ghosts against the frame.

This was Jessica McKeen's place. She was another friend of Amanda's. I figured that she might know Emma too. I opened the door of the minivan and stepped out. It was cold. Snow was piled in dirty lumps against the curb where it hadn't yet crumbled to the level of the road.

I crossed the street and knocked on the door. It rattled. A dog barked from the apartment next door. A bike on the lawn was frozen into the grass and somewhere children were crying. The door opened and a woman stood behind it. She was pregnant. Her eyes were nearly grey and had red, tangled lines running throughout them.

"Jessica?"

"Who are you?" she asked, looking me up and down. She was about twenty-five and at least twenty must've been hard.

"Frank Cain."

"What are you? Social services?"

"No. I'm an investigator."

"An investigator?"

"Yeah. I've been hired to find Amanda Foster."

"What are you, a cop?"

"No."

"I don't want any kind of trouble," she said. There was fear in her eyes—uneasiness, maybe.

"I'm not looking for trouble. I'm looking for Amanda," I said. "I'm not a cop," I repeated. "I was hired by Malory Fleet."

"So, what do you want?"

"I want to ask you a couple of questions. It won't take long."

"I don't think I can help you much." Her voice crackled as she spoke.

"That's ok."

"Go on then."

"How well did you know Amanda?" I asked. A light breeze swept the street, drawing leaves from the ground and causing them to spiral.

"Well enough."

"You were friends?"

"Yeah."

"Any idea where she is?"

Jessica laughed. She clearly wasn't happy that I was here, or with the line of questioning.

"Did it surprise you to hear that she disappeared?"

"Surprise me? I don't know. I wasn't expecting it. She's not from here, though. Maybe she just went home."

"She didn't really have any family at home."

"She didn't have any here, either."

"I guess not," I said. I hoped that I wouldn't have to go to Moncton but I knew that I likely would before it was all over.

"Her boyfriend died," Jessica said, looking at me. She was steadier now. "I don't want to say it but... she disappeared on the anniversary."

"What does that tell you?"

"Must've been a hard day, that's all I know. Maybe she couldn't handle it."

I'd considered it myself. The police must've too. But it was all speculation with Jessica, anyway, and I had a real lead elsewhere, so I decided to move on. "Do you know Emma McLoughlin?" I asked.

"Not really," she said. "I've met her. She's nice but her boyfriend's a real piece of shit."

"What do you mean?"

"He's a piece of shit."

"They all are," I said. "In what way, specifically?"

"He's just a prick. I've known him a long time. He messes around on her."

"How do you know that?"

She shrugged. She was leaning against the doorframe with her arms crossed. Baby toys were scattered across the ground on the floor behind her.

"Does she know?"

"I think so."

"You have any proof?"

She looked back into the house for a second. "He sleeps with my cousin. He goes by her house most mornings before work. That proof enough for you?"

"Who's your cousin?"

"I'm not getting into this," she said. A baby started to cry inside. Jessica looked back into the apartment. "I gotta go."

"That's alright," I said. I had enough already.

She looked out through the gap as she closed the door. "I hope you find her," she said.

I was sitting in Malory's house looking at the picture of Amanda on the table. I don't know why I was there because I knew I wasn't going to tell her anything anyway.

"You want something to drink?" Malory asked.

"No," I said. "That's alright."

"Coffee, or something?"

"I'm good, thanks."

Malory sat still on the couch. I felt sorry for her but I was starting to realize that she didn't know half of what she thought she knew. I didn't know who to believe.

My own mom was a nurse. She was left alone when my father died. She tried to fill the emptiness but the man she met was as bad as any other. I remember those days too easy. The rumble of the pickup in the early morning was always the first sign. By the time the sun dropped, there would be tears and there would be screaming. There might be sirens. There might be blood.

The forest near my house was thick, the soil damp and healthy. Leaves and pinecones scattered throughout. Unlike at home, life there was balanced. Squirrels, insects, birds, deer, and mushrooms. They all had their roles and they filled them. I'd lean my rusty bike against a tree and sit beside it, close my eyes and listen to the rustle and hum. The vibrancy of life in the forest melted together and could not be broken down.

Sometimes, Dawn came into the forest and we sat together, safe and sound. I met Dawn on the first day of school. She was my first friend. Maybe the only real friend I ever had. She had it like me at home and we didn't have to say anything. We spent a lot of time together when I was young. One day, Dawn did not come into school. She never came back. I never knew why.

Something about Malory reminded me of her. And I guess I was thinking about Dawn because she had disappeared too. It was one of those mysteries in life.

The cat rubbed against my leg. It hopped up onto my lap and I let it settle in. "If you had to make a guess, where would you say she went?" It was just something to say.

Malory picked up the frame and stared. "I don't know," she said. "Where would you go?"

"If I had to disappear?"

"Or wanted to."

I thought about it for a while. "I'd leave the country," I said. "The province, at least. What about you?"

"If I could figure that out, I'd have been out of here twenty-five years ago," Malory said. She put the picture down.

"When did you find out that she was missing?"

Malory didn't look at me. "I can't remember."

"You can't?"

"Not exactly," she said, looking up. "At first, I thought she might've just been avoiding me."

"Why would she do that?"

"I don't know. It might've been too much for her."

"What might have been too much?" I asked.

"Everything. Things were intense after Jason died. There was a lot of emotion. A lot of trauma."

"So, you didn't find out right away?"

"When did she go missing?" Malory looked up at me.

It felt like a trick question. "A year after Jason," I said. "Halloween 2016."

Malory shook her head. "That's when I reported it." She paused. "Nobody knows when she went missing, or where she went missing from. She just vanished." She picked up the picture and stared at it again.

"Someone knows," I said.

Her eyes flicked to me so hard I thought she'd get whiplash. "Who?" she asked. The cat jumped out of my lap.

"I don't know," I said, slowly. "Someone must."

I saw her interest fade. "That's why I hired you," she said. "To find out."

"We will." Suddenly, I felt the need to act busy and checked the time. "Alright," I said, "I'd better go."

"Call if you hear anything new. I'll be waiting."

I went out and closed the door behind me. I could feel her eyes on me as I crossed the street and got back into the van.

In the South End, I pulled over to the side of the road and took out my phone. When I made the call, it rang twice. "Tommy. How're you doing?"

"Not bad. What do you need? You meet up with Boucher?"

"Yeah," I said. "You know him at all?"

"Not well. Why?"

"What do you know?"

"Little heavy handed," Tommy said. "Some word that he's linked up in bad ways. No real evidence—that's just the word around the station. Why?"

"Nothing," I said. "Just trying to get a read on him."

"This what you're calling about? I won't sell info on another officer, crooked or not."

I found a new angle. "Listen, I need an address."

There was a moment of silence. "That's an act offence," he said, referring to the rules of the Police Act.

"I know it is. I'll pay you extra at the end of the month."

"Who are you looking for?"

"Emma McLoughlin," I said. "She works at Service NB."

"Alright," Tommy said. "I'll give you a call in a few."

"Thanks, Tommy."

The line went dead. I put the phone down and rubbed my hands together to warm them up. I adjusted the angle of the vents and turned on the radio. Shifting into drive, I pulled out onto the road. There were few cars on the block, so there was a fairly easy path. I went up the street and turned to cross the causeway, heading for the Tim Hortons. The fog was so thick it crept up along the edge and lapped at the road ahead. Beyond the concrete barrier was a never-ending sheet of grey.

I turned at the lights and pulled into the lot. I went through the drive-thru and got a double double and a chocolate glazed. Then I parked up near the road and waited for the call. I couldn't even see the cars passing on the road, just the white glare of headlights. Again, I thought about the fact that nothing seemed to be adding up. I hoped that Tommy could help me out. The phone rang.

"Frank?"

"Yeah. Who's this?"

"Detective Boucher."

"Stuart." It wasn't the cop I was hoping for. I put the coffee in the cup holder and wiped the crumbs away from my mouth. "How's it going?" I wondered if he'd seen me earlier.

"Good," he said. "I just wanted to follow up on our meeting. You have any luck tracking that girl down?"

"No," I said. "Not yet."

"Have you spoken to Malory again?"

"Yeah."

"What did she say?"

"What do you mean?" I tried to peer through the fog. Though I couldn't see it, I knew that there was a line outside the Chinese restaurant across the road. It was always the same, rain or snow.

"Did you tell her you spoke with me?"

"Yeah."

"And she didn't say anything?"

"Like what?" I asked.

"I don't know. Like I said, she's crazy."

"Anything else you can tell me about the girl?" I asked. My phone beeped. I took it away from my ear and looked at the screen. "Hey, Stuart, I've got another call coming in. I gotta take it."

"Alright," he said. "Give me a call if you find anything. The case is still open."

"Right," I said. I hung up and took the second call.

"Frank, it's Tommy."

"What's up?"

"I got that address. Thirteen Tower Street."

I thought I knew where it was—a little out of the way, but not too far. "Is that West"

"Yeah."

"Thirteen?"

"That's right."

"Alright. Thanks, Tommy."

"No problem, buddy."

I hung up the phone, backed out of the parking spot, and went out onto the road, lights throwing glare to the fog. Visibility was just mere feet ahead. I had to hope there was no one on the road because if there was I'd hit them before I knew it. Occasionally, shaky red lights seeped through the fog.

Fog that thick is difficult to describe. It sits like a grey-white screen, solid in the distance. And the distance is not far. All you can see are the few scrapbook images close enough to stay ahead.

After a while, I reached the street and parked up at the intersection closest to the house. I had to creep forward to find the house number, then retreat once I did. It was a nice house. A real home. I shut off the lights and sat back in the van. I listened to music and looked at a picture of Madison on my phone. She was on the shore. Waves crashed on rocks behind her. Clouds hung low.

The ocean sky has presence. I remember nights when the earth was just an accent. Madison and me and the sky. On a stormy night, shifting black forms swelled. Lightning flickered silently, casting lingering light in the grey. Only then could you really see the sky for what it is.

I looked up at the house. The form barely cut through the fog and the night was growing dark behind it. In the morning, Emma's boyfriend left first. James was driving an old silver Accord. When he turned at the end of the block, I turned the key in the ignition and started the car. It was early: 5:30. The roads were empty except for dock workers and labourers.

The air in the van was a little sharp so I lowered the window. The morning was sharp too. I followed the Accord to Millidgeville. Rock clawed through hills along the road. It was like living in a quarry. He stopped outside a house there, looked over his shoulder, and went up to the door. I checked the time: 5:45.

A woman answered and I knew that I had him. I took my pictures as they went inside together. She was a girl, really. She was good looking and gave the impression that she hadn't gotten out of bed to stay out of bed.

At 6:15, he left the house. I waited until he started the car and then turned the minivan across the road, blocking the way. He stopped. I got out and walked around the hood of the van to his passenger side. He lowered the window. "The fuck, man?"

He was thick. There was little doubt about that. I leaned on the window. "How's your girlfriend?" I asked.

"What?"

"Emma," I said. "How is she?"

He looked closely. His soul patch twitched. "Who the fuck are you?"

"Private investigator," I said. I held up the phone and showed him the pictures.

His hand shot forward. The seat belt held him back.

I stepped back, shaking my head. "Don't worry," I said. "I won't show Emma. I just need you to tell me one thing."

"Get fucked, buddy."

"Wrong attitude."

"The fuck do you want?"

"Amanda Foster," I said.

"What?"

"Where is she?"

"I don't know. What the fuck are you talking about?"

"Where's Amanda?"

"The fuck do you care, anyway?"

I didn't reply. I held the phone in my hand so he couldn't forget. I didn't like the guy. I kind of wanted him to get out and try something, but I also knew it would be a lot easier if he didn't.

"I don't know where she is," he said. "No one does."

"You know that's not true."

"I seen her once in my entire life."

"Where is she?"

"I can't tell you," he said.

"Then I'll go take these to Emma."

"Those?" he laughed. "You've got nothing, bud. Move your shit-can out the road."

"That what Emma's going to think? She know this girl?" I glanced up at the house. The girl was standing in the front window by then, looking out.

The boyfriend swallowed. He chewed his lip. "She's in Norton," he said. "Now, get the fuck out of the way." He started to roll up the window.

I stepped forward, putting my hands on the rising glass. It was a bad idea—the window kept rising. "Where in Norton?" I asked. "I need an address."

"If I see you again, I'm gonna kick your ass."

I took my hands off the window just before it finished climbing. I saw him looking in the rearview, so I went back over to the van and opened the door. The Accord tore past, riding the curb.

I shifted and turned the van around, hit the gas and followed him to the end of the block. Then another little bit to give him a scare, before turning back towards the core.

If he was telling the truth, Amanda Foster was less than an hour away.

PART III

Saint John was a lonely place.

Through the rain and fog, it wasn't even possible to see across the harbour from Tin Can Beach. It was silent except for the rolling wind and the occasional horn coming through the fog and rain. I stood on the rocks looking out to where the sky and water disappeared into one another. The wind cut through my jacket, a damp chill that settled and stayed.

Madison told me that there was a cop, years before, who brought poor boys down here on cold nights to keep himself warm. It was a story and a legend and the truth. He was caught and he was free.

Partridge Island was out there. I used to try to imagine what it must've been like for the Irish who landed there during the famine. I used to imagine ships bobbing black in the swell of the harbour, the skeleton of rigging and masts without sails. I imagined bodies on the decks, living and dead. Fear and relief and the stench of both.

Then one day I went out to St. Mary's Cemetery at the edge of the city and saw the overgrown tangles hiding faded and crumbling markers, thousands of bodies rotting beneath in anonymity, and I stopped imagining anything at all. I figured that if the Irish didn't care then neither should I.

I turned away from the harbour, thinking about Stuart Boucher. He was a cop, and a cop was a certain type of man. He was a certain type of cop, too. I hoped that Amanda hadn't seen him at his worst.

Madison had liked that I was distant, capable of solitude. She craved independence and I gave it to her. Her ex was a jealous type. He watched her. Took to parking outside her home to see who came and went, to see who she met with. He'd text ten, fifteen times a day, whether he received a response or not. He'd been controlling, abusive. They all were. It was a habit, a pattern.

We used to come down to Tin Can Beach in the mornings and watch the fog roll in across the water. It came high and heavy. That was when we talked about the things that mattered. I don't know what we talked about the rest of the time.

A chain link fence, stripped bare of chain, its frame browned with rust, protruded from the frozen grass. Two crows sat on the cross-bar looking down to the black water. I turned and went back up the rocks to the parking lot and walked along the broken road to the park. I stopped at the intersection in front of her apartment, watching. As I stood there, I knew that I was as bad as the rest.

That car was parked out front. The lights were out in her apartment and I knew what that meant. It was a grey Volkswagen Passat. I looked over my shoulder and crossed the road. It was early still. The streets were quiet. Those who were out at the hour would not care. I took a picture of the plate.

She'd told me about her dad on Tin Can Beach, a violent man capable of great compassion when the mood struck. The first time we fought was when I said I'd kill him if I met him and she told me that I had no right to say that about her father.

I looked down at the license plate number in the picture and then slipped the phone back into my pocket. The window above was still dark. I went across to the park and sat on a bench. The metal bars were wet. Rain and meltwater gathered in divots. Fog was playing around the statue in front of me. Looking across at the front door of her apartment building, I waited for the man to appear.

The damp cold hardened beneath my coat. I was planning to call Tommy to get the name the plates were registered to when the sun came up. I didn't know what the plan was from there.

I've only gone hunting once in my life. In some ways, it's a lot like being an investigator. There's a lot more waiting around than you expect. We were hunting coyote. The boys said it was because they were pests and predators and a nuisance for the livestock. Really it was because the boys wanted something to kill in the winter and they'd likely admit it if you asked them more than once.

We drove out in the early morning in a pickup, sloshing in dirty ruts, and parked up by the edge of the woods near the beds. In the snow, coyotes are easy to track. There were three of us. Two of the boys had calls and all three of us had rifles.

It was early morning and our breath was hanging in the air before us. We set up stands in the bushes and sat with thermoses. It was quiet and peaceful and I could smell the branches around me. They warned me that you could go ten times and not take a single animal. We sat out for a long time watching the day unfold. Eventually, the coyotes came out to the calls. There was no decoy so they ran straight to the sound. Guns punched over the snow and coyotes fell. There was a lot of waiting in between.

Later, the carcasses were discarded. I didn't pull the trigger but I helped dispose of the bodies. When we were done, we drove straight to the bar and got drunk. I smelled the blood on my hands every time I tilted the bottle.

This was a sickness. The realization struck me as I sat there in the park in the early morning. There was something inside me that needed to go—something in my nature, or so engrained that it was close enough to it. I took out my phone and deleted the picture of the plate.

I needed to let her go.

I stood up and walked across the grass to Charlotte Street. From there, I made my way up to Princess and back to the office, the long way around. At the office, a black car was parked out front and the engine was running. Stuart Boucher was visible through the windshield. Seeing him pass by may not have been a coincidence after all. For some reason, I felt like I needed to run. But I could see that he'd already seen me, so I kept walking. When I reached the car, he opened the door and got out.

"Frank."

"Detective Boucher. How are you?"

"I'm alright," he said. He was standing in the dim light. Shadows cut his face at odd angles. "Making any headway on that case?"

"Doing what I can," I said. "Feels a bit like trying to untie an old rope that's been knotted too many times, know what I mean?"

"You want to show me what you've got?"

"It's not much," I said.

"You never know what can help an investigation."

I glanced at the front door. "Don't you need a warrant for that?"

"Not if you give me permission," Boucher said. His tone shifted. "Unless there's some reason you don't want to."

"I'm working a case," I said. "This is confidential stuff."

"I'm a cop," he said. "Trust me, no one else is going to see it."

"You know how fast we'd be out of business if our clients thought we were giving information to the police?"

He was standing close. "You have something you don't want me to see?"

"It's not like that."

"I threw you a bone when you needed it," he said. "Help me out here."

I stood my ground. "If I find anything, I'll give you a call."

For a moment, it looked like he was going to hit me. He stood tall with his jaw clenched. His chest felt about six inches closer to me than his face. Then he turned and walked away. He got back into the car, slammed the door, and started the engine. Light flooded the street with the engine's growl.

I watched the car pull out onto the road and disappear, drawing the glow away with it. I went up into the office and sat there with the lights off, wondering what the hell was going on.

Amanda was alive in Norton, as far as I could tell. It hadn't even taken much digging for me to get that. I opened an old phonebook and flipped through the pages. There were two Fosters in Norton. I had a hunch that I'd find her with one or the other. It seemed dead simple.

I looked up through the narrow windows. It was too dark to see over the curve of the road to the plateau of the harbour, where the fog gathered and rolled. Rain began falling, drumming on glass and crackling on the road. The rush was sudden and loud. It was dark and grey. A figure, dark and shiny in the rain, was walking down the middle of the road between slick black cars. With the hood pulled up and hands in the pockets, it hardly looked human. It was nothing, really. Just somebody going about their business in the rain. Still, I couldn't stop thinking about it. It didn't take much to veil humanity.

As quick as it began, the rain stopped falling. I'll admit that I was scared. If Boucher was involved somehow, he had a lot to lose. He also had a lot of power to make sure that didn't happen. I didn't believe that anyone was crazy. Crazy just meant you didn't have to understand or even try.

Twenty minutes later, I was still sitting there. There were footsteps and then the door opened and the lights came on. Randy jumped when he saw me in the corner. "Jesus, Frank," he said.

"Sorry. I got here early."

"You eat breakfast?" Randy asked.

"No."

"Hungry?"

"Yeah," I said. "I am, actually."

He nodded and stepped back out into the hall.

That was the way of men sometimes. They didn't talk a lot and liked to leave you feeling uneasy because that's the way they felt themselves. I followed him to the door, turning off the light as I passed.

We went to a diner a few blocks away where the food was cheap enough to make you wonder. We took a seat at a clean table near the back in view of the windows. Randy picked up a plastic menu with teeth marks around the edges.

"Take a look at the Colter file yet?" I asked.

"No," Randy said. "I haven't had a chance. Think it's good to go?"

"Yeah. I got a few shots of him at the VLTs in the middle of the afternoon."

He smiled without looking up. "That should cinch it."

"Yep."

"How's the other thing?"

The waitress came over. She was an older lady with a practised smile. "Can I get you started with some coffee?" She gestured with the pot in her hand.

"Yeah," Randy said. "Black. Thanks, hun."

"Black for me too."

She filled the mugs on the table.

"I think we're ready to order too," Randy said.

"Shoot."

"The basic breakfast. Scrambled eggs and white toast."

"I'll have the same," I said.

"Keeping it simple." Her voice rang with an elevated service tone. "I'll be right back with that for you."

"How'd that job go?" I asked.

"The dentist?"

"Yeah, the infidelity."

"It was easy." Randy picked up the coffee cup. "I think he wanted to get caught."

"Why's that?"

"He wanted to leave her but didn't have the balls to do it." Randy sipped his coffee. "Megan says if a man hasn't cheated he just hasn't had the chance yet."

"She says that to you?"

"She does."

"Do you think that's true?"

"I think it's close enough."

Randy let his eyes follow the young waitress at the table beside us. A few moments later, our own waitress came back and set down two plates. Eggs, bacon, sausage, and toast.

"That was fast," I said.

"We keep things rolling," she replied.

I pierced my eggs with a fork and watched the yolk spread. I'd asked for scrambled but at that speed I didn't care. "So, do you think she's going to divorce him?"

"No," Randy said, smiling. "She wants to try to work it out."

We finished eating and Randy paid. I didn't mention Boucher to him because I didn't want him to panic and drop the case. I didn't tell him about Amanda either and I can't really say why. I just didn't know what the right thing to do was yet.

When we left, Randy went back to the office and I placed a call to Malory. She didn't pick up. From there, I began to wander aimlessly. A man I knew, Lee, was pacing in the alleyway next to the market in a haze, alone in the world. It was the first time I'd seen him in months. He'd probably been inside.

When I first moved to Saint John, I saw him all the time. He wasn't homeless. He was a street person and the streets were his home. Lee used to sit in the park with a yellow Tilley on his head, telling whatever joke he'd learned that morning to anyone who'd listen. They were always bad.

One day, he got arrested for mushrooms. He breached probation and ended up in jail. When he got out, he was addicted to meth. Since then, he'd been lost to a perpetual state of decay. I didn't bother trying to say hello and went in through the doors of the market.

I moved absently through the thin passages between the stalls looking at the trinkets and food. Even though I'd just eaten an hour before, I was hungry. I realized that I hadn't really been eating at all over the past few days.

The sandwiches at the deli were too expensive to justify, so I walked a little further. Then stopped. Boucher was at the far end of the market, looking at fruit. He was with a young girl, ten years or less. She was smiling and looking up at him and if he noticed he didn't let on.

It was his daughter and she loved him. It was immediately clear. Adoration encompassed her.

I thought about what Malory had said and hoped for a moment that he hit his wife and not his child, because at least she'd understand what was going on. Then I realized how sick I was. How sick it all was.

I turned and walked down the aisle, back past the deli, to distance myself. I didn't want to see and I didn't want to be seen.

He was a father. I had not considered it before. Not only that, but his daughter loved him. That's the nature of life.

I don't know much about fathers, to be honest. I was told that my father died lobster fishing. I've also heard that he was meeting a shipment of drugs on the bay. Either way, he disappeared into the grey silence of choppy water on a rusty fishing boat, just trying to scrape by. I never knew him. Maybe if I had it would've all gone a little different.

The snow was deep. The minivan could barely handle the dirt roads. The sky was blue and the rolling hills were white. Red barns and white farmhouses dotted the land. I turned up the little road past the first farmhouse and slowed, trying to read the number but couldn't see it. I kept driving further. The next house was about half a kilometre up. They became a little more frequent after that.

I slowed the van when I reached the house I was looking for. It was on the hillside. The van struggled to climb the driveway's incline in the snow. When I made it to the top, I pulled up alongside an old red Ford Ranger. I looked down at the page from the phonebook. There were two Fosters in Norton and this was the first.

I stepped out of the car. The air was cold and still. The packed snow crackled and squeaked beneath my boots as I walked up to the front door. A woman was parting the curtain and peering through.

I knew immediately that it was her. She looked scared as hell. I waved so she wouldn't have an out. A moment later, the door opened. She did not speak. Her eyes spoke for her. She was small. She had deep brown hair and a plaid shirt. She wore no makeup—a change from the pictures I'd seen.

"Amanda," I said. "My name's Frank. I'm a private investigator. I was hired by Malory Fleet."

She swallowed. "How did you find me?"

"It's my job," I said.

"What do you want?"

"I haven't told Malory where you are," I said. I still didn't know what the right thing was to do or say, so I decided to ride it out for a while. "Can I come in? I want to talk to you."

Amanda looked at me for a long time. "My uncle's out," she said.

"I can wait until he's home, if you want."

"Come in," she said, shaking her head. "It's cold as hell." She moved away from the door and I stepped through. The house was tidy. We were in a small entryway between the kitchen and the living room. Stairs led up to the second floor and a hall led back past the kitchen. I took my boots off and followed Amanda into the living room. I sat down on the couch but she stayed standing.

"Why didn't you tell Malory where I am?" she asked.

"Someone told me that you didn't want to be found," I said.

She nodded. "I like Malory but she's too much. I'm not her daughter."

"I know."

"I'm not hiding from her but she's a talker. She can't help herself."

"Who are you hiding from?" I asked.

Amanda didn't reply. She shifted nervously. "You want something to drink?"

"I'm alright."

"I've got beer in the fridge," she said.

I realized that she wanted one. "Yeah, alright," I said. "I'll have a beer."

Amanda went to the kitchen and opened the fridge. I took my coat off and threw it over the back of the couch. I looked around the room. There were tools and books and knick-knacks lying around. The window looked out down the hill to the road. White fields rolled to pines.

Amanda came back with two bottles of Alpine. She handed one to me. It was cold. My hands were still cold so I set the bottle down on the table. This time, Amanda sat across from me. It was hard to believe that she was here.

"Are you going to tell the cops?" she asked.

"Should I?"

"They think I killed Jason," she said.

"I heard that."

"What do you think?"

"I really don't know but I'd be surprised," I said. "Maybe I'm just sexist."

"It's not sexist," she said. "Men kill women. Women kill men who kill women."

I didn't respond.

"I didn't do it," she added.

"How long have you been out here?"

"About six months."

I could hear the washing machine running through the wall. "This is your uncle's house?"

She nodded.

I picked up the beer and took a drink. "Why are you hiding, if you didn't do it?"

"I'm not scared of the charges," she said.

"What are you scared of?"

She hesitated, then answered. "The cop."

"Boucher?"

She took another drink.

"Why?"

"He's crazy."

"I've been hearing that word a lot lately."

"What would you call it? He wouldn't leave me alone. He started stalking me, harassing me. He called every day, parked outside my house, threatened me. I had to leave."

"Did you report him?"

"To who?" she asked.

"What did he want from you?"

"I don't know," she said. "He thought I killed Jason for some reason and then he just got obsessed with me. I thought he was going to kill me." She paused. "I thought that you were him when I heard the knock at the door."

"Who killed Jason?" I asked. I needed her to give it to me straight. I needed something concrete.

"Bikers, probably," she said.

I was surprised by how direct it came. "He was in trouble with them?"

"I guess."

"He worked with them?"

"Everyone does," Amanda said. She paused for a long time but I knew to wait, and eventually it paid off. "Including Boucher," she added.

"Boucher works with bikers?"

"That's just my assumption. He was entirely against looking into them."

"Do you have evidence of that?"

"No, but I have common sense. And, bikers have cops on their payroll. How else could they walk the streets in their jackets identifying them as active criminals?"

"Why would the bikers kill Jason?"

She was silent for a while before she answered. "I think they thought he was a rat."

"Why?"

"I don't know. Somebody was talking. A couple guys got arrested." She looked at me. "Jay wasn't a rat."

"Tell me about him," I said. I don't know why I said it. It was a risk but I felt the need to understand.

"What do you want to know?" she asked.

"Whatever you want to say."

She looked at me for a while and I thought she wasn't going to say anything at all but then she started talking.

The first time she saw Jason, she had an overwhelming compulsion to know him. There was something about the way he carried himself and the way he stood in the kitchen with no deference to anybody. He said something and the boys around him laughed. He was the one they all wanted to be. It was a Halloween party, a day that would prove inescapable. Then again, she knew a lot of people who met at Halloween parties. It made sense because everyone was playing pretend and that was the nature of most relationships anyway.

Something happened at the party after he'd caught her eye. Someone came to the house who shouldn't have been there and a row broke out in the kitchen near the back door. She didn't see him hit the guy—when she looked over, Jason was laughing and the other guy was already out the door. What she saw was the way the other boys looked up to him and the way he smiled. She knew he was tough but it was kind of a second-hand knowledge. She hadn't seen him hit the other guy and didn't really have to face it, so she liked that too.

She approached him and everything she said made him laugh. When the party dispersed, they stayed together. It was simple after that. They never got bored and one morning she woke up and realized that they'd spent every day together for two weeks. She couldn't remember what it felt like to be alone.

Amanda stopped talking. She was looking out the window behind me. There were tears in her eyes. "And now he's gone," she said.

There was something familiar in the story and it made me like her. It was a story of love and truth. I saw that she knew what mattered in life. I wondered if she'd known before it was gone. I didn't want her to stop talking so I threw another log in the fire. "Tell me what happened that night," I said, "so I can get my head around this thing."

On October 31st, 2015, Amanda was standing at the counter of the little apartment. She was drinking a gin and soda and wearing a cat suit, because they were hosting a party that evening. It was pretty early and Jason was out meeting some of the guys.

Rae Sremmurd played from the speaker on the counter. She bent down to take the popcorn machine from the cupboard and took a bag of popcorn from the cabinet. She plugged it in, poured the kernels, and put a bowl in front of the spout. When she hit the switch, the motor started running.

The apartment was clean and she had a few decorations out—streamers and spiders. The neighbours were arguing again. She hoped that they'd stop before the party started. If not, some of the boys might end up going over and it could turn ugly.

The machine started popping but the noise drowned out the music, so she shut it off. As she sipped her gin and soda, she heard three thunderous pops right outside the window. She sat up straight. They were gunshots. She'd heard them before but never so close.

The glass slipped from her fingers and hit the floor, shattering. She rushed to the window on the other side of the kitchen and looked down to the street. Jason's car had pulled up along the curb outside at an odd angle. Three holes in the windshield; a cobweb of cracks.

She finished the beer and set it down on the table.

"And then you called Malory?" I asked.

"I ran outside and found him in the car. Then I called Malory," she said. Her voice shook but she didn't waver. I imagined her standing there in the aftermath of gunfire.

"Why did you call her and not the police?"

"He was a dealer," she said. "What was I supposed to do? Even if the cops are crooked, they still don't like dealers they don't work with."

"Who called the police then?"

"A neighbour."

"What happened then?"

"The cops showed up. They were there for days. The whole block was shut down."

"When did Boucher arrive?"

"I don't know," she said. "He might've been there the first night but I don't remember meeting him until the next day."

"At the apartment?"

"I went and stayed with Malory. He showed up at the door and brought me into the station for questioning."

I picked up the beer and took a drink. "What kind of things was he asking?"

"He asked about the broken glass in the kitchen and why I didn't call the cops. He asked if Jason ever hit me and if I felt like taking revenge. He thought I had something to do with it from the first."

My phone rang. The number was private. "One second. I better take this," I said. I answered the phone. "Hello?"

There was a muffled noise. The line crackled. The connection was poor.

"Hello?" I repeated. The muffled voice responded again. I couldn't get a read on it. "Sorry, I'm out in Norton," I said. "The signal is really bad. Can you call me back in about an hour?"

There was another muffled noise. I hung up.

"The drawbacks of country life," she said.

"Sorry," I said. "Where were we?"

"Boucher."

"Right," I said. I hesitated. I wasn't always the best with people. "When did he start harassing you?" I asked. It seemed blunt but, if she cared, she didn't let on.

"A couple months after that, I guess. They didn't really have any leads, other than bikers. Maybe he was getting worried. He started coming by a lot, asking a lot of questions."

"What did you tell them about the bikers?"

Amanda hesitated before answering. "I didn't want to rat on anyone. I said that I thought it might've been bikers during one of the interviews but even the other cops didn't think it was them. They thought that bikers wouldn't do it out in the open like that, so early in the evening."

"Bikers don't seem all that subtle to me."

She picked up the empty bottle and fiddled with it. "People go missing. They don't usually find the bodies."

I wondered how she knew. *How much* she knew. I finished the beer and set it down.

Amanda picked it up. "Want another?" she asked.

I looked at my watch. It was nearly time to get back. I had her where I wanted her, though, and didn't want to let it go. "Yeah," I said, "why not."

Amanda disappeared into the kitchen again and came back into the room with two cans. She handed me one. "It started to get really bad about six months after they killed Jay. Detective Boucher was kind of nice at first. Like, cop nice, you know? Like, he thought it was me but was polite about it. Then it started to get aggressive. He showed up all the time. He followed me around. Sometimes it was other cops but usually him. He started calling ten, fifteen times a day."

"Fifteen times a day?"

"I had to change my number. Then he got the new one and I got rid of my phone completely." She sipped the beer and looked out the window behind me. "He told me that it was just a matter of time. He said that Jason's partners would want revenge so I'd better turn myself in. After I moved in with Emma, he backed off for a little while. Then he broke into the apartment."

"He broke in?"

"Yeah. No warrant. Just on his own. I was at work. The neighbour across the road saw him. He broke the back door and stole my laptop."

"Jesus," I said. "Did you tell anyone about this?"

"Yeah," she said. "Emma knows. Malory, too." She took another drink. "I ran into him at a bar one time and he was really drunk and followed me into the bathroom. He cornered me in the stall and got, like, right up in my face. He grabbed me by the throat. I was so scared. I thought he was going to kill me."

"When did you decide to leave?"

"Right after that. I told Emma I was going and packed a bag. I stayed with her for the night, then I came down here to stay with my uncle."

"Why didn't you tell Malory?"

"I wanted to get away," she said. "I didn't want to bring it all with me. I guess that wasn't really possible. She reported me missing on the anniversary of Jason's death. I guess she was having a hard time. I'd already been gone for weeks by then."

I looked at my watch again. It was time to go. "Look," I said, "I'm sorry but I have to go."

I really had to think about this. It didn't seem fair to put her through any more hardship. "I'm not going to tell Malory that we found you. I haven't even told my boss yet. I'm going to get him to drop the case and leave it at that. Maybe you can get some peace."

"Thank you," she said. She looked truly grateful. "How is she?"

"Malory?"

"Yeah."

"I don't know," I answered honestly. "I don't think she'll find peace anytime soon. Maybe the search keeps her going."

"Maybe," Amanda said.

I picked up my coat and put it on, then my boots. "I'll see you," I said.

"I hope not," she replied.

I gave a small smile and shut the door. I got into the minivan and started the engine on the second try. The wheel was cold. I blasted the heat, turned the car around, and went down the hill to the road. I pulled out onto the highway and drove in silence, leaving the radio off. It was a quiet drive. There were almost no cars on the road. I moved through the fields and farms. Forest grew up along the highway.

I believed every word she spoke. The right thing to do was to let her live in peace. It was the same thing I wanted, after all.

I was thinking about Amanda and Jason and then I started thinking about me and Madison. It wasn't a big leap. Jason was dead and Madison was gone. There was more to it than that, I think.

After about twenty minutes, I reached a long bend in the road. The bend carried over a hill. The lanes were close and I was wary of my speed in the snow. I could see down over the rolling fields and forests. Asphalt tendrils enwrapped the earth, cutting through snow and snowy pine, entrails strewn across unmarred beauty.

A murder of crows scattered across the road. As I neared, the birds took flight, cast from the earth with force. Wings thrashed as the cluster dispersed. They spiraled above. A single crow remained on the road. Its wings spread wide, reaching out in both directions. It was low to the ground, slumped. The lower half of its body was injured, somehow.

The crow could not take flight. Aware, the other birds flurried, swooping in panic. The distance closed. The uninjured birds tore back into the sky. I was unable, unwilling, to swerve in the conditions. I bore down on the crow, waiting like a crucified man. I saw helplessness in its black eyes before it disappeared beneath the van.

I did not feel anything. I only knew that I hit it because I saw it spread across the road in the rearview. It's easy to get used to road-kill. Slumped figures dot the roadways. Sheer carnage, shredded carrion: fur and flesh and feather. People draw lines of desensitization—a deer, a cub, a cat.

As I rounded the bend, a car passed me going the other direction. It was a black sedan and it was moving fast. I got a brief flash of the driver in the front seat. He had short, cropped hair. He looked across at the van as he passed. He was familiar.

I slowed and looked in the rearview and watched the car disappear around the bend. I drove on a little further but my chest was tight and I couldn't stop thinking of Amanda back in Norton and Stuart Boucher, and the phone call that I had received from a private number.

I slowed the car and did a U-turn on the empty highway and hit the gas hard, heading back in the opposite direction. I tried not to look when I drove past the scattered organs and innards of the crow. The van was poor on the roads and started to slide. I kept my speed as high as I could but didn't see the car on the highway again.

When I reached Norton, I pulled back up the gravel road past the blue farmhouse and followed it up to the Foster's. The sky was growing dark overhead.

I turned up the hill and struggled to the top. The black sedan was parked at an angle beside the Ranger in the driveway. The house was dark. I left the engine running and ran to the house. I didn't bother knocking. As soon as I threw the front door open I could hear the struggle in the living room.

Amanda was lying on her back over the coffee table. Boucher was looming over her with his hands around her throat. There was a pistol holstered on his side. She was kicking and struggling for breath.

I yelled something. It sounded weak.

Boucher looked over and loosened his hands on her neck. "Stay out of this," he said, his eyes ablaze. He let go with one hand and pointed. "Get the fuck out. Not a fucking word."

"Let her go," I said, stepping into the room.

Boucher let her go and moved towards me instead. I tried to ready myself but he hit me with a hard right hand before I could. It was sharp. I went backwards and hit my head on the floor. My vision flashed white and dark clouds crept in at the edges. I sat up and tried to clear my eyes, blinking. My head throbbed and my ears were ringing. Slowly, the white faded.

The world returned. Amanda tried to hit Boucher with the Alpine bottle but he caught her arm and twisted it down. She screamed. Then a shadow passed over the hallway. I looked up.

A man with white hair was standing in the doorway with a hunting rifle. He was wearing a flannel jacket and an orange toque. He looked down at me and then at the detective. He raised the rifle and said something. The detective moved towards him.

The rifle clap filled the house.

We drove out along the riverside like a caravan. I was in the minivan, Amanda took the sedan, and her uncle drove the pickup truck.

There were two gas cans in the back of the sedan. There was a canvas tarp wrapped around the body in the back of the pickup. I thought that we should use something better. The uncle said that canvas would allow it to decompose. It made me wonder how he knew.

We headed out along the side of the river as far as the cars could go. We parked beside the bridge and then walked on foot under the cover of darkness.

The snow was heavy. The woods were thick. The sky was black. We trudged for hours. I could not keep track of where we were going. I stumbled, disoriented and lost. It was probably for the best. My boots soaked through. Wet cold burned my feet. The wool socks were grating and raw. By the time we stopped, I was sure that I was walking in my own blood.

We dropped the canvas tarp. The inanimate thud was sickening. My shoulders ached with the release. I drove the shovel into the snow, soft and easy. Then we hit the ground and it was frozen.

My hands were numb. Sharp pain surged through them each time the pointed edge of the shovel attempted to break through the frozen surface of the earth. I thought that I would lose them to frostbite. I thought that we had gone too far, that it would be better to give it all up. That it would be easier to lie down and wait for the thaw.

We dug for hours more. Silence stretched around us, black and frightening. In the hollows of the woods, the slightest sound echoed, disrupting eerie stillness.

When I peered through the bare and twisted limbs, terrified that someone was out there looking in, I saw the depths of my soul. The vast emptiness of the north was nothing like this. Madison had been right to go.

Soil spread, spoiling the snow cover. Where the snow had melted, gnarled roots clawed through. The hole was deep. We lifted the tarp and threw the body in. The canvas slipped open, exposing the pale skin beneath. I threw the first shovelful of earth down onto his face in an attempt to hide it. Black dirt landed on pale skin in wet clumps. I didn't have the strength to vomit. When I looked at Amanda, I recognized the fear in her eyes. Her uncle was without expression. We continued to throw dirt onto the body until it was buried. It was the longest moment of my life. My muscles burned from the toil. It went on and on and the world around us was black and cold and frightening.

When he was buried, I did not feel any better, just the same sickness inside, the same revulsion at it all. Something was clawing at me from the inside, trying to break free. I was glad that he was gone but even the dead and buried can rise to the surface. I knew that I would forever wander in a vacant haze, terrified of being discovered.

It was near morning before I got back into the minivan and drove up onto the little bridge, heading back towards the highway. The sun was shining and the skies were clear. My clothes were torn and wet. I drove with the radio on, thinking about the dockyards of Saint John.

The closer I got, the less snow covered the ground.

I needed to report back to Randy. I needed to tell him that I had not found Amanda. I needed to tell him to close the case.

In Saint John, sunshine was rare.

I drove in, past front steps where people huddled and smoked, dockyards where people worked, park benches where people slept. I drove into the heart of the city, where it was dark and cold and grey clouds rose from cracks in the road.

When day broke, I was still hunched over the steering wheel, staring up at the window above. The window was a yellow patch in the haze. Randy was in there because the lights were on and he was always in at this hour. I needed to go in and stay composed. I needed to tell him to drop the case.

But there was guilt on my face. I knew it was there because I could feel it in my heart. I was scared of what would happen when I opened my mouth. There was only one thing that could really come out and it was the same thing I couldn't say.

I pulled back out onto the street.

The whole drive up all I thought about was getting out and getting clear. It wasn't until then that I really started to think about the man we'd buried in the dirt. Thinking about him as a man, that is.

Malory had said that they solved 50 percent, the ones that were easy. I didn't know if that was true. When a cop got killed, they solved it. I knew that much.

I started to think. What if he was right? What if Amanda had done it? She didn't even need to do it herself. What if she didn't love Jason and set him up to be killed that night? Or, what if she was in love and that's why she needed to do it? In the end, it didn't really matter. I was here and he was gone. I had to keep going.

I think I'd been planning to drive to Malory's when I pulled out onto the road but as I drove I realized that I couldn't go out there either. I needed someone disconnected from it all, someone who could make things ok again. I needed someone who understood me and would know how to make it right.

When Madison stepped out into the cold morning, the look on her face was not the one I'd hoped to see.

"Frank?"

"Hey, Madison."

"What are you doing?"

I leaned as nonchalantly as I could on the hood of the van in front of her apartment building. "I wanted to see you," I said.

"What the fuck, Frank?"

I took a step towards her. "What's wrong?"

The realization was sudden. "Have you done this before?" she asked. "Have you been watching me?"

"I miss you."

"You've been scaring the shit out of me."

"I love you, Madison."

I knew the words were hollow as soon as they left my lips. Saying it aloud made me finally realize that it wasn't true. I was clinging to something I should have dropped long before.

She laughed. It wasn't the laugh I remembered. "We dated for two months, Frank. You don't love me."

"How can you say that?" I was now just asking out of habit, or fear.

She looked scared. "I'm asking you to leave me alone, Frank," she said. "I'm telling you that I need you to stop this."

I waited for her to regret what she said. If she did, she didn't show it. I stood there until the apparition I'd built up suddenly crumbled and the real woman emerged out of the smoke.

"I don't want to call the police but I will," she said.

She meant it, and it would have been the right thing for her to do.

"Ok, I'm going," I said. "Goodbye, Madison."

She didn't reply and I didn't wait for it. I got back in the van. Tears were trying to break through but I don't think it was all from her, if I was honest with myself for once. Nothing was going to be the same anymore. Everything was going to be different, forever.

I took out my phone. It was still pretty early and I had two missed calls, both from Tommy. It had all come to an end.

When I left Madison's, I started to think about Amanda and all the things she'd told me. I turned around and went back out to Norton.

The van sloshed in dirty ruts on the road, the snow stained brown along its edges. Farmhouses stood crooked on the hills. The phone rang. I lowered the window and cast it out into the snow. It didn't make it all the way and landed in the dirty slush.

I passed familiar scenes, then pulled back up the gravel road past the blue farmhouse and followed it up to the Foster's. I struggled up the hill and parked beside the red Ranger in the driveway.

Before I got out of the car, the curtains parted. Then the door opened and the uncle was standing there looking at me like he'd never seen me before. I got out of the van and walked towards the house.

"Amanda here?" I asked. I didn't like the sound of my voice out here.

"She's gone." He spoke without emotion.

"Do you know where she went?"

"No." He hitched his thumbs into his belt loops and looked past me. "She's gone. It would be better for all of us if you forgot about this."

"I need to talk to her about something," I said. "It's important." I stopped in the wet snow in front of the stoop and put my hands in my pockets.

"I'm not joking, son," he said. "You'd best forget this." A rifle leaned against the wall behind him. He didn't close the door but just stood there, looking past me, waiting. I remembered the house shaking with the clap. I looked at anything but his eyes.

I turned and went back to the van. Down the long drive to the road, I punched the wheel to stop myself from crying.

The city was cold. Wind cut deep coming in from the water. The sun was gone and the sky was dark. The clouds were low and shifting.

I was too scared to go home because that's where they could find me. I didn't have anywhere else to go, so I sat in the van down the block and waited to drift away, bottle on the seat beside me.

It took a long time. The numbers on the clock wouldn't change. Maybe it was too cold and they were frozen. I didn't know if that could happen. All I know is that it went on forever and then it was over.

In the morning there were no cars on the block. It was a good sign but the relief was fleeting. There was something on the news. It was not what I expected but it was a bellow for restless fear all the same. The body of a man had washed up in Manawagonish Cove. They found it tangled in the reeds at Saints Rest.

I knew it wasn't Boucher because he was buried in the dirt in the forest and I'd put him there. I couldn't help but make the connection anyway.

They wouldn't find the body. Even if I wanted to, I couldn't lead them to it. I wondered what would happen when the seasons turned, what the thaw would bring. I started to think about him out there, decaying, and I had to move again.

That night, I went to a motel. The sun stained the sky as it fell behind the pine ridge. It was the warmest night for months.

I used to sit out long after the sky had gone from blue to pink and deepened past blue again. I'd sit silent in the dark and listen to the owls, and some nights it felt good to be alone. The stars would appear, nervously at first in the absence of the sun, but eventually with a confidence and brightness and giddy lustre that solitude could never bring, and I'd change my mind about everything.

That night, I didn't bother sitting out. When the sky went dark, I got into bed and let the tears run onto the pillow. Because I was alone, I didn't bother trying to stop them. Sleep didn't come for a long time. Eventually I knew that I'd drifted off because I found myself waking up again.

I entered a pattern: losing consciousness briefly and then returning from the vague and shapeless void. I sweat a lot. The sheets were damp when I woke and the air was cold and I shivered. Being enwrapped again was a comfort.

When I pulled from it—the throbbing haze of restless sleep—I lay there for far too long. In the dark at night, time stopped working right sometimes.

Then the cycle repeated. Back into darkness. Sometimes it felt like I had been gone for hours and sometimes it felt like no time at all. Everything that had happened had already happened and was gone. Every second forward was new and pure and unlived. The walls spun and the red numbers on the alarm clock jumped back and forth, hours and minutes, or sometimes stood still for far too long. The sweat kept flowing and my arms kept shaking in the cold damp sheets.

I woke again. The room was silent and still. I turned on the light. A fly was trapped in the lampshade and this set it off. It buzzed and rattled against the fabric walls; its shadow cast through in the light so it looked much bigger than it actually was. It stopped and sat still momentarily before taking flight and battering itself against the incidental cage once again. I knew that birds could tire themselves to death trying to get through a window. I wondered if flies were the same.

The alarm clock on the nightstand read 2:45 a.m., but that couldn't be right. I hadn't checked the time when I got into bed but I'd been there for hours—awake for hours and asleep for hours too.

I was thinking about Boucher and Madison and myself. Mostly myself. I thought about the body in the weeds at Saints Rest. I thought about that endless slumber.

In the morning, I drove past Madison's place. It was early and the sky was still dark. It was cold and my breath hung in the air. The Passat was parked out front. A man sat in the driver's seat; his face lit up by the blue glow of his phone.

What happened next is a blur but I do know I got out of the car and then I had the door to the Passat open and my hand tangled in his collar and I hit him in the face. I felt soft flesh and the give of the jaw. They pretend it hurts to punch a man but it feels pretty good unless you hit him in the brow. I hit him again. He slumped in the seat—the only thing holding him up was me—and I hit him again and again as the ding of the open door expanded into the air.

Then I was back in the van. The steering wheel was loose and thin but it felt good to drive. The van rattled as it tried to trace the bumps in the road. I knew that I couldn't just keep driving around town. Eventually they'd pull me over. It was the company van and Randy knew I had it.

There was a man in the weeds at Saints Rest. I couldn't stop thinking about him. I was coming up with theories and connections and starting to feel like I was crazy. I needed to get out before it all closed in or the great tumult consumed me entirely.

I drove up to Union and began to head east. It started to rain as I crossed the causeway. A few sharp pellets on the windshield and then a solid flow. By the time I pulled into the gas station on the other side, it was coming down heavy. I got out and stood in the shelter as the rain fell on everything else. The air was cool and damp. There was a sign on the pump that said, *Pay inside.*

When the tank was half full I took the nozzle and replaced it in the pump. Leaning back on the van, I caught the moon wavering through the rain. The bulb above the pump flashed, turned off, and then buzzed slowly back to life. I crossed the parking lot and entered the store. The lights inside were bright but flickered, as fluorescent bulbs do. The attendant was young and bored, barely glancing up with the rattle of the door, before looking right back to his magazine. I wandered the aisles of snacks and car-care products aimlessly, picking up a bag of pretzels, carrying them for a while, then returning them to a shelf where they didn't belong. I poured a coffee from the machine. The tap sputtered.

Gas station coffee. It was the same as thermos coffee. The coffee of hockey rinks and jobsites, of all-day-breakfast diners, nursing homes, after-hour clinics, and waiting rooms where I sat after school and watched sick and scared people come and go until my mother came out from behind the off-limit heavy doors, a blur of scrubs behind a steam cloud of strong smelling, weak tasting coffee in a cheap Styrofoam cup.

I handed the attendant some bills. They gave me my change and said that the weather was rough. I agreed but as I walked back through the rain to the van and watched the light glisten on the pavement and the grass reach up to meet the rain, I decided that it wasn't rough at all.

From there, I took the backroads. I left the city behind and everything I passed I recognized, including a little white cross in the ditch, protruding from the slush. There was something written on it, I don't know what.

The sky was not separate from the world, hanging above as it usually did, but had opened up with rain and fog so that the road, the rock, and the earth itself blended and faded into it. The evening hung on and for a time the forest seemed endless. The steady roll of trees and grass and signs and rocks and nothing I hadn't seen before. I turned on the radio. The signal was bad, but the song was good. The wipers worked tirelessly— just enough to provide glimpses through the downpour. Even then, I could only see feet ahead before the smoky, throbbing shroud took over, beckoning me forward.

And then I passed through it.

Like a wall, I passed through the rain and fog and entered another world. I put the window down. It smelled like manure and soil and stickiness: fresh, real life. The dark remnants of cloud shrank in the sky and it was blue. Snow lay across the earth. Fields and forest stretched far.

I drove until I reached a bridge that felt right. Then I stopped the van and left the engine running. I went across to the cold metal railing and leaned on it, looking out. The air was hard, the sky open and clear. The river and rocks were buried beneath ice and snow. There was a bird in the sky, distant and black. It circled, alone and free. I felt a sense of calm. A great calm. I looked out across the unmarred blanket that rested so definitely across the earth and felt nothing but an inexplicable sense of absolute calm. I continued to stand there because I knew that the moment the air shifted the darkness would return and consume me entirely.

From the bridge, the riverbanks stretch into the distance, narrowing, until they pinch and close, succumbing to forest. The sun is low and cold. It is somewhere there, along that stretch, that the body is buried. I don't know where.

# ACKNOWLEDGMENTS

The following names represent just a few of the people I'd like to acknowledge. If I could, I'd list far more. Barring that, I'd first like to thank Heloisa (Helena), one of the most remarkable people I have ever met. Helena, the sheer amount of kindness that you shared with me during the most difficult time in my life was more powerful than I can ever express. I thank my dad, Gerard Beirne, for working with me through a lot of the editing and expansion of this book after my injury. I also thank Robin Philpot and Leila Marshy. Robin, for his personal support, enabling me to publish three books before the age of thirty, and also for the tremendous press which he has created, publishing fiction and non-fiction which draws attention to vital but often overlooked issues. Leila, you played a vital, often invisible role in the creation of this book and I appreciate it immensely. I would like to thank Cliff Turner for giving us permisson to use his painting "Fog Lifting" for the cover. I would also like to thank Arts NB (New Brunswick) and the Canada Council for their support.

Additionally, I thank the staff at the Moncton Hospital and the Stan Cassidy Centre, for the incredible compassion and care that I received from them all. Finally, I would like to thank Dr. Dhany Charest, who saved my life.

ALSO FROM BARAKA BOOKS

MY THIEVERY OF THE PEOPLE, STORIES
by Leila Marshy

LOOKING FOR HER by Carolyn Marie Souaid

DEAR HAIDER by Lili Zeng

THE THICKNESS OF ICE by Gerard Beirne

EINSTEIN ON ISRAEL AND ZIONISM,
NEW ENRICHED EDIITION by Fred Jerome

A JEW IN RAMALLAH AND OTHER ESSAYS
by Carla Blank

EYES HAVE SEEN, FROM MISSISSIPPI
TO MONTREAL by Fred Anderson

Printed by Imprimerie Gauvin
Gatineau, Québec